New Found Land

Herbert F. Hopkins

W&W

Words and Wood Publishing

W&W   Words and Wood Publishing

www.wordsandwood.ca

©2017 Herbert F. Hopkins

ISBN 978-0-9813429-4-8

A CIP catalogue record for the book is available from Library and Archives Canada.

B.W. Chubbs: cover art and illustrations.

For Jane

Acknowledgements

Susan Rendell is the Wizard of Worddom. I salute her flawless editing and exquisite writing. From the fullness of my heart, thank you.

Having Boyd Chubbs as a collaborator is a joy. To have his work for my cover is an honour. Thank you, Boyd.

Crown prosecutor Phil LeFeuvre, lawyer Bob Buckingham, lawyer Randy Piercey, and Royal Newfoundland Constabulary constable David Emberley (joint RCMP/RNC drug task force) all helped me to understand legal jargon and court procedures. Thank you, gentlemen.

To the Goliaths at the Office of the High Sheriff, particularly Mike and Chris, thank you. Glad you are on my side.

To Jerry Cramm, site manager of Gander International Airport, thank you for the tour and the stories.

Though often obscured in cigar smoke, Jim Moore has always been there with clear advice. Thanks, buddy.

To my meticulous first readers, Randy Piercey, Phil LeFeuvre, Lynda Boyd, James Moore, Boyd Chubbs, Jane Dennison, Malcolm Rutherford, Blake Cryderman and Linda Andrews, thank you for your vision—both kinds.

In his 1993 novella, "Waking Up in the City of Dreams," Bryan Hennessy coined the phrase, "City of Dreams." I've been using it ever since. Thanks for the loan, Bryan.

Thanks to my wife, Jane, who supports me in every way, and encourages me when the chips are down. Jane's love and positive energy are inspiring, and her curry is to die for. At sixty, like me, she realizes that life has just begun.

Lastly, thank you, readers—you are the final chapter. Stories are incomplete without you.

"Let us pretend in order to make the pretence into a reality."

—C. S Lewis

t was St. John's Eve and Angéline LeBlanc was standing on the Magnolia Bridge over Bayou St. John. Fort St. Jean was just upriver. The name of Angéline's Newfoundland home seemed to be everywhere in New Orleans.

She was swaying along to the drums with the rest of the white-clad worshippers on the footbridge. The old walking bridge seemed as organic as the water that flowed beneath it. Angéline had been here so many times before. Too bad Papa was so old and stuck in his ways; he could be here with her, in a white suit and top hat. She smiled at the thought.

The young woman beside her stopped singing long enough to whisper, "You look lost, *sha*."

"Lost in thought," Angéline whispered back, turning her head to look at her companion in the ritual.

"I'm Rosella," the woman said.

"A beautiful name."

"Thank you. And yours?"

"Angéline, Angéline LeBlanc."

"White angel."

"That's right."

A blonde woman leaned over a makeshift shrine in the middle of the bridge and lit some candles. Like the entire congregation, male and female, she was dressed in white, and her head was covered in a white kerchief. In the middle of the shrine was a statue of the famous voodoo queen, Marie Laveau. Around the statue were piled gifts: wine, hair, ribbons, barrettes, candles, flowers and *gris-gris* bags.

Angéline leaned towards Rosella and whispered: "She is so lovely, Mambo Sallie."

The voodoo priestess raised her arms skyward. A snowy egret flew overhead.

A drummer played an African rhythm while another man tapped an axe head with a machete. The congregation began to sway, locked together by their arms and their belief. A chant welled up from deep inside them:

> *Papa Legba ouvre baye pou mwen, Ago eh!*
> *Papa Legba ouvre baye pou mwen*
> *Ouvre baye pou mwen, Papa*

Angéline could feel the energy build as they called on the keeper of the gate, Papa Legba, to open the portal to the spirit realm so that the *lwa*, the spirits, could come down. The fingers of Angéline's hands pinched the outer layer of her long white skirt as she swayed from side to side like a pendulum. Her own spirit seemed intent on flying out of her body to meet the spirits halfway. The spirits were in the breeze, in the birds, in the stars that were coming alive. The drums were in her chest; her heart and mind were soaring.

Rosella leaned over and placed a kiss on Angéline's cheek. Angéline took her hand and squeezed it. How comforting to be here once again, with her fellow *voodooists.*

"Such a beautiful ring, Angéline. Where did you get it?"

"A gift from my boyfriend. The stone is labradorite. Have you ever heard of Labrador?"

"Not really."

The drums died away. Angéline opened her half-shut eyes and watched as Mambo Sallie knelt next to Marie Laveau's shrine. Rosella pulled a purple cloth bag from her left pocket, a *gris-gris* bag. She approached the shrine and loosened the drawstring; a heap of objects spilt onto the shrine: a blue flower, a lodestone, dust, a feather, a red ribbon. A piece of paper also fell, landing face up; the word *angel* had been written on it seven times, each "angel" connected to the next, and the first connected to the last, in a full circle.

Angéline felt a sharp jolt: she had forgotten to bring gifts for Marie. She had come all this way and had nothing to give. The ring, her beautiful ring; it was all she had. But she had promised Luke she would never take it off, it was the symbol of their bond, their life together. It made her feel connected to him in ways she hardly understood. And it was beautiful, bought from a street vendor a world away. Thick silver, it was soft and hard at the same time. It felt solid on her finger; she liked the weight and the way the light played on the multicoloured stone, making the colours change. It reminded her of Luke's eyes. The shrine's candles added their light to the stone, and it blazed as never before.

Luke owned the ring before he gave it to her; he used to twist it when he was nervous. Sometimes he turned it round and round his finger while he read a poem he had just written, so in fear of her response that he could hardly get the words out.

She noticed she was twisting the ring herself now. Just one more go round and the ring would slip past her knuckle. She felt the release and looked down: it had fallen into a bouquet of white flowers.

Rosella whispered in Angéline's ear: "You are near the crossroads—we will go together."

Angéline felt as if she was on a threshold; it was like being at the edge of sleep, ready to fall into a dream, unaware of herself, her ego. The material world had vanished with her ring: it meant nothing. "Papa Legba, Papa Legba."

A cross appeared in front of her, hanging in the air. A cross at the crossroads.

Cross, crossroads, where is this place? The bayou was still there, but it was now a spiritual world, where consciousness was no longer a state of mind but an elation of the soul. Time and space were gone, the weight of life had disappeared. Angéline was suspended on a swing at the edge of up and down. When she closed her eyes a valley appeared, a river ran into the sea and a great white egret soared overhead. The primal beat of a drum sounded throughout the valley. She had arrived at the cross—the crossroads.

With both hands, she reached out to the valley. *Cross, crossroads—I'm ready.*

2

Luke Delaney doubled up a piece of cardboard and wedged it under one leg of the barroom table. Everything seemed off kilter. He wondered if he'd ever be happy, always wanting something that was just out of reach and not even knowing what it was. At least—no, at best—there was Angéline. Even though a short skirt could still fondle his thoughts, he wasn't tempted. If he and Angéline so much as touched the same branch together when they were berry-picking, Luke could feel the connection between them. That kind of love didn't come along every day. Never, for most people.

Tonight, though, he was spending time with his old friend Mossy. A few pints and a couple of stories. Lies, Mossy called them. Sometimes they played the guitar and sang, Luke taking the melody and Mossy singing the high harmony. The top notes seemed counter to Mossy's size, but then everything had a surface that belied reality.

It was a Friday night at the Ship, a pub on Solomon's Lane. The lane was named after Simon

Solomon, a watchmaker and jeweller who had been
the first unofficial postmaster of Newfoundland,
making his own stamps by hand. The place was still
about communication, but by song, poetry and prose
now; the Ship was the centre of worship for the arts.
Late at night, Bill, the bartender who loved Tom
Waits, would allow him to growl through the stereo
speakers and send you home singing his tunes. But
not before you talked to the smokers outside, who
were inhaling fresh air and an assortment of dried
leaves. A bright red awning hung above them like an
umbrella, but other than looking good it did little else;
in this city, the rain squalled from the side. The
painted floor of the Ship had been chafed clean by
the soles of a million shoes—wild women and men
shaking in the night. The Ship had the best stage in St.
John's, maybe the world. It was one of the few things
in the City of Dreams that never changed. Artists
came from everywhere to play the Ship, but mostly it
was local acts, strutting down over the hill to bury
themselves in the night. The sound was always good; a
big man took care of that. He seemed to live there,
fitted into a corner in front of his board. Backstage

was a kitchen, a tight muddle of fridges and fryers. Barely enough room to turn a phrase. Some of the Ship's performers blossomed, others died on the tree and some fell from grace. But everyone came back.

Luke liked the hand-painted mermaid that graced a support post. He believed this post held up the city. If it fell, so too would the City of Dreams. But tonight, the post was not even holding him up. He was in a rotten mood. His head was throbbing. Everything was annoying him. And a woman at the bar wouldn't shut up. Three rum and Cokes hadn't even begun to put a dent in it. He needed something else, but he didn't want to think about that.

"Hey, Mossy; sorry, I'm just not into this. Going to make my way home." Luke leaned towards Mossy and made a vague gesture towards the rest of the crowded bar. "You enjoy."

"Aw, come on, Luke—stay for one more."

"Naw, I'll finish this and be gone. I just don't feel right. I'm a little lost tonight." Should he tell Mossy? Not now. Maybe not ever.

"Angéline?"

"No, we're good. Listen, this is just a funk, melancholia, whatever. It will pass."

"Perhaps the fault is in your stars, old buddy. I've got a friend who's into astrology. Interested?"

"Don't think so. Not really into that shit. Anyway, I'm going. I'll give you a call tomorrow."

"Okay. Take care, Luke."

3

Caleb Buckle never worried about the night. Day, night, it was all the same to a blind man. Memories got him around. He knew all the streets and the coves by heart, but it was the alleys he'd played in as a kid that he knew best. East and west were easy; the wind almost always blew from the west and when it didn't Caleb knew from the feel of it where it had come from. The southwest wind was best, up from southern waters, warm and humid and strong. North was cold and came from up the hill. An east wind was even worse, like the old saying went: "When the wind is in the east, 'tis neither good for man nor beast." But he and his beast, Blackjack, made out okay no matter which way the wind was blowing. Blackjack was a boxer cross, white from tip to tail. Cops ignored the off-leash dog; no one had ever complained about him. "Caleb, Blackjack, how's it going?" was a common Water Street refrain.

Before Caleb lost his sight, he had sung country songs in bars around the bay with Blackjack for drinks and tips—just like the song said. Despite being blind, or more likely because of it, his voice had gotten better; thick as cream, someone said. But getting gigs in the city was a pain, and he didn't like the late starts; besides, no one wanted a ratty old mutt around. So instead of having the people come to him, he went to the people. He made more money on the streets than he had in the bars—over a hundred a day sometimes. And no liquor bill. Only once did someone try to steal his money, but Blackjack had taken care of that. Word travelled fast: you'd lose your hand if you stole from the blind man.

The day was closing in. It didn't really matter to him as long as he was dry. Right now, he was beside a building that had a ledge or an awning above it; something that was trying to keep out the drifting rain, anyway. He didn't mind being outside most of the time; in fact, he liked it. Sometimes in the summer he even stayed out all night, on a bench or on the ground with a couple of blankets. The fresh air made him sleep like a dead man.

"Caleb—over here, it's Luke."

Caleb felt Blackjack stiffen and then relax. "Jesus, Luke, sneaking up on a blind man. Lucky you still got your nuts. Got something for me?"

"Yeah, the usual."

"The usual's just fine. Thanks, Luke."

The handshake was short. Luke was reminded of the first time he'd met Caleb. It had been in McMurdo's Lane, when two thieves had stolen his wallet and phone. Caleb had overheard the encounter and set Blackjack loose. The men had run off, leaving Luke on the ground. When he'd looked around to see where all the barking was coming from, he could hardly believe his eyes—saved by old blind Caleb's dog. Luke's back had hurt like hell, he couldn't move and his vest had been ripped off him.

"Should I shout for help?" Caleb had said.

"No, just get me my vest, please; it's right there by your left foot. There's two pills in the inside pocket, and I'm going to need one of them." Luke always kept two pills with him; he never knew when the pain might hit.

Luke had watched Caleb kick around until he'd found the vest, picked it up and slipped his hand into the pocket. Watched him hesitate and fondle the pills before he handed them over. Luke had managed to summon up enough saliva to swallow one of them. It took twenty minutes to kick in, and by then he had dragged himself over to a set of concrete steps. He had given the second pill to the blind guy, as a way of thanking him. Luke had figured the old man would take it home, crush it up and snort it; that was the way to get the heroin-like high. He remembered thinking that if he were blind and homeless, or even one of these things, he would do the same. There were days he thought about trying it anyway.

4

Angéline felt warm and light, as if she could soar across the sky. She lifted her heels, then her toes—she flew, faster and faster. But then she began to fall. "Help me, Queen Marie! I am your child, please help me!" She kept falling. Faster and faster, nothing could stop her now, not Marie, not Papa Legba, not Rosella. Not Luke, who was so far away.

When she hit bottom, her bones splintered, her skin ripped apart. But she was not in her body; she was above it looking down. And beside her, there was a presence; someone or something that exuded peace and unconditional love. She turned her head: a gigantic snake, Li Grande Zombi, sat beside her, its golden eyes deep pools of intelligence and compassion. Beside the snake stood an old black man, smoking a pipe. "Papa Legba, can you help me?" She felt all the sorrow of her heart flow out towards the old man as she spoke the six words. Papa Legba replied; Angéline heard with her mind, not her ears. *You must ask your papa what to do,* sha. *He is trying to help you, but your heart is too full of unhappiness; he cannot reach*

15

you. Look for him in small things, with an open and clear heart.
The snake moved closer to Angéline; she reached out
and stroked its warm, dry skin. And then she was
falling again, through a cold black void. She screamed
and screamed, but no sound came out; it was like
trying to scream underwater. Then there was a jolt,
and her head hit something cold and hard. She put her
hand up and grasped the object; it felt familiar to her.
She opened her eyes: she was on her bedroom floor in
St. John's, Newfoundland, with her hand around the
leg of the bedside table.

Angéline lay on the king-sized bed looking up
at the white plaster mouldings on the ceiling. This old
house on the South Side was supposed to be their
sanctuary. And it was. But it never felt like it on the
days when she had the dream. The dream always laid
her low; bad thoughts followed it. Thirty thousand
from Luke's father's will had covered the down
payment on the house, but now work was sporadic
and money was tight. The worst thing, though, was the

way Luke was acting; did she even know who he was anymore? She groaned and pushed her aching body deep into the fleecy sheets.

There was a noise at the front door.

"Luke, is that you?"

"Yes. I'll be right there, honey."

Luke poured himself a glass of water and took it with him upstairs. The bedroom door was closed. He opened it: Angéline was sitting upright in the bed, white-faced and anxious-looking.

"Jesus, Angel what happened—are you okay?"

"I'm all right, Luke. It's the dream. I fell out of bed this time." Angéline grimaced, or perhaps it was a wry smile. Luke sat down beside her and put his arm around her shoulder.

"My God, Angel. We need to do something." But what do you do about nightmares? Luke wondered if she should see her GP again. He didn't seem to know much about trauma, though, and that's what the dream was all about, wasn't it? The trauma of the accident, the trauma of the deaths and her other losses?

"For now, Luke, just hold me. I'll be okay. But, yes, I will talk to somebody. Again." I need to speak to Mambo Sallie, she thought. I need to find someone like Rosella in this place. Someone to guide me.

Luke put both his arms around her and held her tight, trying to squeeze his love into her. She sighed and relaxed against him.

"The only thing I have on tomorrow is a meeting, in the morning, with some doctor at the university. She wants to talk to me about my addiction—some kind of study or something. We can spend the afternoon together." He kissed her on the forehead. "Whatever it takes, Angel, whatever it takes. I'm with you."

Was he? Angelina wasn't sure where Luke was these days. She sighed and squeezed his hand. She thought about what Papa Legba had said to her—Papa Legba or her own subconscious. If only she could confide in Luke about her dreams, and how much she missed her spiritual practice with the others back in New Orleans. All she told him was how the dreams affected her; he would never understand about Queen Marie and Papa Legba, and the deep connection to the world through her soul that voodoo gave her. He did understand how much she missed her father.

5

Doctor Liliana Sánchez was sitting behind the old oak desk, scrolling through her email while she waited for the knock on her office door. The new off-campus office, a large room in a tastefully renovated old hotel, was a haven from the swarm of Memorial University students. She was tops in her field, and everybody wanted a piece of her brain. Her new office also boasted a million-dollar view of the harbour and the city; seabirds regularly flew past the windows. Today a pale afternoon sun was warming her bare arm and part of her face; she reached up and started to tuck a strand of her black-and-grey hair behind one ear.

A firm but polite knock sounded at the door. Liliana liked the sound of the knock; it helped her to start sizing up the person she suspected—hoped—was waiting to see her. She stood up and stretched, then went to the door and swung it open. A tall man who appeared to be in his late thirties or early forties stood in the corridor. He had a clean-shaven, kind face and curly hair; the battered old hat he was wearing struck

an incongruous note, but she already knew that he
had, as they said, "issues."

"Come in. Luke Delaney, right?"

"Yes, Luke Delaney."

"Nice hat."

"Thanks, long story."

"Looks like it's been around the world."

"Yeah, you might say that. It's Armenian, my
grandfather's."

"Very cool."

Luke looked around the room; a framed
diploma hung next to the coat tree. It was in Spanish,
but he figured it said she had a PhD.

"So, what do I call you? Professor? Doctor?"

"Liliana is fine."

"Nice digs." Luke moved towards the window.
He looked out over the neat little bowl of ocean
cupped by the old city. He never tired of that view, the
way the wooden houses looked like steps on the side
of the hill. Still, though, progress was leaving its ugly
mark. Oil had reinvented the oldest city. The skyline
seemed to change with the seasons. The wooden
houses had fallen victim to gentrification, Gutted,

slicked up, divested of their individuality, they now cost ten times what they had a couple of decades ago. He would like to live downtown, but unless things changed, the other side of the harbour was as close as he would get. Getting rich didn't seem plausible. But you never knew: sometimes the extraordinary lurked behind the humdrum.

"Quite the view."

"Isn't it? But I'm so busy I rarely get much time to look out the window. So, Mr. Delaney . . ."

"No, Luke is fine. My father was Mr. Delaney. I have a long way to go to deserve that title."

"I'm sorry. How long ago did he die?"

"It was two years in October. Medication screw-up. My mother died six months later of a broken heart. Cardiac arrhythmia. They were a pretty tight couple."

Liliana patted Luke's shoulder. "Sometimes death can be a kindness, you know."

"I know. But it was hard on me, both of them more or less at once. Only child and all that."

"Have a seat." Liliana indicated a low glass table surrounded by three chairs in the far corner of the room. Luke sat down in one of the chairs and Lillian took a seat across from him.

"Okay, then. So why am I here?"

"I'd like to help you with your addiction."

"Why me?"

"Because I know you enrolled in some detox trials at MUN and they didn't work for you. According to the files, you seem to be a strong, intelligent, responsible person who would stay the course of treatment I recommend.

"Luke, as you know, addiction is complicated. What makes one person an addict will have no effect on another person. Genes and environment play a part, but we certainly haven't got addiction nailed down. Or its cure. You have an addiction to opiates, Luke. I'm sure you've done the research, so I'm not going to go into it.

"For nearly twenty years I've been working on a different kind of approach to addiction, a different kind of fix, and I'm ready to start trials. Would you like to hear?"

For an instant, Luke returned to the crash scene: the signpost splintering, Angéline's bloody head against the windshield, letters flying in the wind. Had it been ten years?

"Tell me about your fix, Liliana."

"It starts in Havana . . ."

6

Caleb Buckle woke up to the sound of pedestrians making their way to work. He rolled over in his sleeping bag and stretched his arms. "Still fucking dark," he said to Blackjack. Too bad no one else was around, to applaud the humour. He slid out of the bag and got to his feet.

It was a fine day indeed. The dog nosed him in the leg, and Caleb bent down and scratched him behind the ears. Then he felt his way to the dumpster; behind it was the plate and bag of dog food and a leash in case he needed it.

After Blackjack had his breakfast, they headed to Vitamin C, a coffee shop on Water Street. He tied the dog to a parking meter and went into the shop and asked one of the waitresses for a bowl of water, which she was kind enough to take out to Blackjack. In the back of the café, an extra-large coffee and two slices of toast were sitting on his usual table.

"Hey, Caleb, how's it going?" The man's voice grated on his nerves, as always, but he kept his face from showing it.

"Oh, it's you; the coffee must have killed the smell."

"You're a funny guy, Caleb." The voice descended into a whisper, equally grating. "You got the stuff?"

"Yeah. Nice shine on those shoes, Myrick."

Inspector Myrick looked down. Caleb grabbed his hat.

"Taken by a blind man, ha."

"Fuck you, Caleb. One of these days, someone's going to kick the shit out of you—and I won't be around."

"Don't worry about me, Myrick."

"Listen, Caleb, I really don't give a fuck about you. Where is it?"

"In the pouch under Blackjack's collar."

The two men left the café, Myrick in the lead. He smiled and nodded at the woman behind the cash—Jenny, the owner, no flies on that one—and waited for Caleb to catch up with him outside. Caleb untied Blackjack, and Myrick knelt and pretended to pet the dog. He could feel the animal stiffen under his touch, and hear the low growl. It made him want to

whack Caleb and the mutt with his baton, but hitting a
blind man and his dog wouldn't be a good **PR** move.
If people knew the truth, things would be different.
But then he'd have to look inside himself too. And
that wasn't a pretty story.

7

Angéline reached for her handmade mug, the one Luke had bought at a yard sale, and poured herself another cup of coffee. She loved the Emily Brontë quote on the side of the mug: "Whatever our souls are made of, his and mine are the same."

Angéline and Luke were always looking for the best coffee in the city. Coffee shops were popping up everywhere, and countries that were once a remote name on a map were now part of the morning lexicon: Guatemala, Costa Rica, Cuba, Ethiopia, Sumatra, Cambodia, Uganda. The last bag Luke had bought had been from Haiti; it was Angéline's brew of choice this morning. Her grandmother, Amma Dumois, had been from Haiti. A woman of colour in what was once the richest country in the West, now the poorest. Lately, Angéline had started to think about her ancestral home, about maybe going there and tracing her bloodline. Perhaps someday she would even go to Benin, where it had all begun. It was something more than her olive skin, it was the blood that ran through her veins and the stories she'd heard as a child.

Luke stopped at the shoulder before passing over the short bridge that led to the South Side. The Waterford River was resting, barely moving towards the harbour.

The Portuguese had called it Rio de San Johem, St. John's River; perhaps Gaspar Corte-Real had seen the river in late summer when it was a placid stream where John the Baptist might have waded to his knees. There was a legend that John Cabot had discovered the harbour on the feast day of the saint, June 24, in 1497, and that the settlement's name came from this event. Whatever the truth was, by the 1520s at least one English map referred to it as the Haven of St. John's. Luke had fallen out with the church, but it didn't diminish the affection he had for John the Baptist. Although he wasn't sure if sticking to your opinions was worth your head on a platter.

Luke pulled away from the shoulder, crossed over the bridge and stopped at a crossroads. Staring him in the face were the South Side Hills, where his decade-old dream of a wind-driven village never happened. Bills and life had gotten in the way. There was little time for dreams now. Sometimes he wished he had been raised with a hammer instead of a pen; at least the income would be steady.

He turned left onto the Southside Road. The old folks called this the up part of the road; down was further east, where the road went all the way to Fort Amherst at the opening to the harbour. Luke and Angéline lived in the up section, close to the city but still separated from it. Luke liked living apart from the city; living apart was like having the benefit of history, it allowed you to see the whole. The old Volvo, called Newton because of her fondness for gravity, suddenly sputtered. Gravity— if they could only harness it— there was a shitload around here. He wondered why it was always the stuff you couldn't see that was most important.

Along the river, the birch stands stood bare and the ground was a blanket of colour. Luke loved the fall, especially a fall with a pocketful of good news. He pulled up to a row of attached houses and stopped at the one with the red door. They had painted it red when they moved in, to go with the deep blue clapboard and to set their door off from all the rest.

Angéline was still at the kitchen table. He could tell something was on her mind.

"Angel–you okay?"

"Yeah, I'm fine."

She got up from the table, reached into the cupboard and pulled out Luke's mug, which was as big as a bowl. She poured the dregs of the coffee into it and added some hot water.

"Luke, I'm missing New Orleans. And the sun. And the dreams, they're killing me. Maybe I can get help somewhere. Louisiana maybe."

"Whatever it takes."

"If I thought it might help, I'd try anything. Even Hadacol."

"Hadacol?"

"Yeah, Dud LeBlanc."

"What in the name of Jesus is a Dud LeBlanc?"

"Cousin Dud. He was a famous relative of ours, back in the day. Dud had a knack for the gab, and his Dixie Dew Cough Syrup and Happy Day Headache Powder became a statewide sensation. He was a shyster, a snake-oil salesman. Then he got a sore toe and went to a doctor, who gave him some medicine that fixed it. The doctor wouldn't disclose the contents, especially to the likes of Dudley LeBlanc, so Dud stole a bottle and made up his own batch— mostly a mix of vitamins—chemicals—and one secret ingredient: alcohol. Dudley called the stuff Hadacol and hit the road, with a travelling caravan called the Hadacol Medicine Show, featuring the likes of Bob Hope and Hank Williams. When Groucho Marx asked Dud what Hadacol was good for, he said, "It was good for five and half million for me, last year." He made millions of dollars off a product that was no more a cure-all than a bowl of gumbo. But still, people believed in it, and lots of them swore it cured every ailment under the sun."

"Must have been good stuff. Where can we get some?"

"All I'm saying is, I'll try anything, just like all those desperate folks who believed in Dud."

"I'm with you, Angel."

She threw her arms around him, her breathing light on his cheek. A single tear rolled from her chin onto his neck and lingered there until the embrace flattened it. He couldn't decide if it was cold or hot, it was just there, making its mark on his body and mind. He wondered if there was anything truer than tears?

She gently pushed him away and stared into his eyes. "But, money, we have no money."

Luke pulled her close again, long enough to comfort her. "We'll find a way. I promise you."

"I don't know, Luke, I just don't know."

He squeezed her tighter, as if he was crowning the love he had for her.

"Whatever it takes, Angel—beg, steal or borrow—we'll do it."

8

Pedro Cienfuegos' nickname was Ciento, One Hundred, because his arrow-straight fastball had been clocked at one hundred miles an hour. When he took the mound at Estadio Latinoamericano in old Havana, fifty-five thousand fans cheered his name repeatedly, but it never lasted long—the game was over in three pitches, sometimes fewer. Ciento was a closer, called on in the last inning to seal a win. And that's exactly where he was tonight. One pitch away from a win. Or a loss. And from La HabanaVieja to Vedado every door was open, the sound of glory ready to spill onto the streets from ancient TV sets.

A fisherman stood silhouetted against the waning moon. He lit a cigar and cast his line. Every evening at six he made his way to the Malecón, Havana's old seawall, but tonight it was more about baseball than dinner. He loved to look at the water and listen to the game on his radio, and dream about playing for the home team. The radio signal was good tonight, and even the cheap cigar tasted sweet. He thought about diving off the wall if Havana won, to revel in the glory of the moment. It wouldn't be the first time.

The commentators' voices crackled through the tiny transistor. They knew the stakes; their vocal chords were stretched to the maximum, as if the end of the world was approaching. But then the end of the world was nothing new, not in Cuba anyway; it had almost come to that in 1962 when international ideologies went to the brink of Armageddon. But it wasn't ideology this time, it was something far more important, *béisbol,* and the fisherman knew which way the Caribbean wind was blowing, as he always did: it was blowing straight towards centre field—a batter's dream. The radio spewed out the last call: "One man on, two out—four to three for Havana! Miguel Ramirez is stepping up to the plate."

Pedro Cienfuegos stroked his green and yellow necklace while he watched the batter, Ramirez, rub dirt into his hands and spit. Pedro wasn't bothered by the man's defiance. Or his look. He placed two fingers across the wide part of the baseball's seam. Everybody knew what was coming, especially Ramirez:

cowhide flying at a hundred miles an hour. The wind-up was long lanky and full. For half a second the city went quiet; a star fell and a gentle breeze brushed a woman's cheek. The batter shook his head and looked at the third-base coach. The coach shrugged his shoulders. It wasn't a signal, unless it signalled resignation. How could anyone hit something they couldn't see? Ramirez unleashed a vicious swing. A spray of spit shot from the umpire's mouth—"Striiike!" A cloud of dust belched from the catcher's mitt. Ramirez's expression was a combination of astonishment, anger and admiration, all of it morphing into something that resembled a grin. Pedro raised his orisha beads to his mouth, kissed them lightly and tipped the bill of his cap. The place went nuts.

The fisherman hid his radio behind a rock and dove into the sea.

Baseball arrived in Cuba in the 1800s, and its steady rise in popularity was fueled by the many young Cubans who went away to study in the United States. It became a symbol of Cuba's growing independence

from Spain. The archaic and barbaric Spanish bullfight
gave way to modern, wholesome American baseball.
Cubans went to the US to play, and US teams went to
Cuba. Even Castro himself played baseball before the
revolution, and supported it heavily afterwards. But it
was played for the glory of the state and not for
money: Cuban players were amateurs with day jobs,
and they were paid only a pittance.

Baseball was everywhere: you were more likely
to get hit with a baseball in Havana than by a bicycle
or car. The city parks were full of men who revisited
every good and bad play over and over under the
scorching sun. But only praise accompanied Pedro's
name. Besides his skill, he had a sacred surname. On
January 1, 1959, Camilo Cienfuegos was the first rebel
to ride into Havana after Castro's guerrilla fighters
overthrew the Batista regime. He was a handsome
bearded man with a large smile and a devout love for
the Cuban people, who loved him back. Most of all,
he was a good man, a man who always put others
before himself. This comrade of the austere Guevera
and the stirring Castro died just after *La Revolución,*
when his plane plunged into the sea. Camilo had also

loved baseball. Camilo the starter, Pedro the finisher. It all made some kind of sense, and the people liked to think there was a spiritual connection between these two big men with the wide grins. Camilo had never been a true communist, just a brave man with a true heart. Maybe Pedro was the reincarnation of Camilo, risen from a fuselage deep in the sea or perhaps from a grave in the woods. There was talk Camilo had been silenced, although schoolchildren still threw flowers into the sea on the anniversary of his death every year.

From a dark corner of the dugout, an old man stood up and limped to the mound. The crowd cheered wildly as Pedro's father, a member of the Politburo of the Communist Party of Cuba's Central Committee, threw his arms around his boy.

The remains of last night throbbed in Pedro's head. He rolled over, expecting soft skin beside him, but no one was there. Women liked him; they joked about his name. Cienfuegos—one hundred fires. "All burning at the same time," they said.

Pedro buried himself under the thin sheet; the roosters and vendor whistles were tearing his head apart. Reaching up, he closed the long narrow shutters. The room darkened, but the street sounds remained. The squeaky wheels of the bread cart seemed to be in the room. The vendor's voice was, for sure. "*Pan y mantequilla! Paan y mantequillaa!*" Bread and butter were the last things he wanted, but he never let the old man down. He got up and checked his throwing arm; it was sore, but not as sore as his head. The taste of rum filled his mouth. He belched and steadied himself against the wall.

His flat, the main level of what had once been a ship captain's mansion, still had signs of the stately. But the stately had suffered from the state's neglect. Rebar protruded like bones from a carcass, and electric wires hung like old clotheslines, kept functioning by knots and tape. His flat had two rooms, separated by a small courtyard.

Pedro looked in the mirror: he was still a dark-skinned Adonis even if he could barely walk. He tried it anyway, moving out into the courtyard and unhitching the big iron gate. A scrawny man with a crumpled leather face greeted him.

"*Buenos días*, Ciento, the great one. Habana loves you."

"No, *amigo*, you are the great one. You bring us bread."

The man grinned, his false teeth too straight for the crooked line of the mouth. "Yes, but no baseball, no dreams. Who dreams of bread? Maybe the hungry, but there are no hungry here."

The man placed the fresh loaf on the wall of the courtyard. Pedro reached into his pocket and pulled out a few pesos, then dug deeper for a tip. The old man took it and moved on. "*Paan, paan y mantequilaa!*"

Pedro went back inside, laid the bread on the counter and returned to his bed. The phone rang. He wanted to knock it off the table. Probably someone from *Granma*, the newspaper.

10

An incoming aircraft jogged Liliana's memory. It was July 7, 1991: she was on an Aeroflot flight, and the plane was descending into Gander. She wasn't fond of flying, but it was better than riding a sketchy raft across the Florida Straits. She'd had a recurring dream about that, which had scared the hell out of her, especially the terrified look in her young cousin Pedro's eyes as the two of them sank beneath the waves. The only other way out of Cuba was flying; she was supposed to be going to Moscow. Her cousin would not have been given permission to go with her, of course: he was twelve. If she defected successfully in Gander, she would bring him to Canada—somehow, someday.

Before her own defection, she had had to prove her allegiance to the Communist Party of Cuba, which had meant joining the Committees for the Defence of the Revolution, the CDR, which she had hated. The CDR was the Communist Party's version of neighbourhood watch: spying on your neighbours to make sure they were toeing the party line. She had gained the trust of the CDR and made friends with the influential. Before she knew it, she had her papers and was flying back and forth to Moscow, which almost always included a refuelling stop on a Canadian island in the North Atlantic. She told nobody about her plans, not even motherless Pedro, who was like a son to her.

Liliana could hardly believe the landscape; it was one big forest, dotted all over with lakes. Her hands were clammy and her stomach uneasy. The fuselage started to shake, and she gripped the armrest with her fingernails. She thought about the raft and felt terror run along the nerves in her arms. Then the plane's wheels touched the tarmac. It bounced, hit again, bounced again. The last hug from her cousin shot across her mind. She'd told him she'd see him soon, but maybe she would never see him again. But the plane levelled off on the runway and ran smoothly until it came to a halt. Her fingers relaxed, and she and the other passengers breathed a communal sigh of relief. They were on solid ground. It was only then that she realized her day had just started. She was about to defect in the middle of nowhere.

Gander International Airport could barely keep up with the number of aircraft converging on the tarmac. At times, more than two thousand passengers could be seen making their way to the international transit lounge. It was mandatory for passengers to leave the plane while it was refuelling, but when the little airport was overwhelmed some flights refuelled with all passengers aboard. If Liliana's flight was one of those, she knew that she would have to try another time. There were already two planes on the tarmac when Aeroflot 673 touched down, but one of them appeared to be readying for take off. Liliana crossed her fingers.

A voice sounded over the speaker, telling the passengers they must disembark while the plane was being refuelled.

All the passengers got up from their seats, some leaving with handbags, others empty-handed. Liliana picked up her purse, stood up and made her way down the aisle to the exit. She smiled pleasantly at the stewardess as she stepped onto the stairs that led to the tarmac. She envisioned herself running, with three or four police officers chasing her. But that wasn't the case; instead she and nearly four hundred others were walking towards the terminal without a police officer in sight. Still, fear was welling up inside her although she also felt a lightness, a coolness—this temperature was *freedom*. For a moment, she wondered about heat and oppression. Here the sun was shining, but it wasn't a suffocating sun. She didn't care about snow, and all the other foreign things she had read about. She supposed she would get used to them, and they all seemed inconsequential when compared to freedom.

The transit lounge was nearly full. Passengers were stretching their arms and legs; some gazed at the vending machines, wishing they had Canadian currency. Havana to Moscow was nearly ten thousand kilometres; a chocolate bar would be divine. It was risky, but some acquired a few Canadian dollars before leaving their homeland. Much of it was spent on one of payphones in the middle of the lounge. Money was pouring into the pay phones like coins into a slot machine. But Liliana wouldn't be making any calls, not yet anyway. You never knew when the CDR was listening or watching. She tried to keep as low a profile as possible. She looked around the room and moved next to a woman with a child asleep on her shoulder.

Refueling would take only forty minutes and time was already running short. The cigarette smoke was so thick Liliana could barely see the four clocks on the wall: London, New York, Moscow, Gander. How ironic, she thought, this little place alongside these famous cities. In a way though, it made sense. For her, Gander was the world, her new world, and Moscow, her supposed destination, was already long forgotten.

A police officer stood next to the door which led to the main terminal. It was hard to fight her past: cops had always been her enemies, not her friends. But she was here at a crossroads, and her past and future were about to part. She turned and looked at the plane through a window: a uniformed man stepped off the metal stairway and approached the terminal. The knot in her stomach was getting tighter and she felt like vomiting. It was now or never. She walked up to the RCMP officer, but despite having practised them a thousand times, the words never came. The officer sensed her distress. "May I help you?"

She couldn't believe her ears. The man wanted to help her.

"Quiero quedarme . . . I want to stay."

The officer had heard it before, but he was always moved by the magnitude of the simple words.

"You mean defect."

"Yes, sir."

"Just yourself?"

"*Sí,* yes."

"Please come with me."

They walked side by side into the central part of the terminal. Liliana was expecting empty walls and an uninviting room, but she found Italian flooring and designer chairs—surprising sophistication. A huge, blazing mural occupied one wall. They walked by a photo collage of celebrity faces: Fidel was there, in his fatigues, the man from whom she was running. She suddenly felt light-headed and very far from home.

The officer lightly touched her back. "This way." He opened the door to a small office.

"Please, have a seat. Your passport?" Liliana reached into a zippered compartment of her purse, took out her passport and gave it to the officer. He scanned the contents.

"Liliana Sánchez, nice to meet you. I am Corporal Robert Noseworthy of the RCMP. What is your reason for defecting to Canada?"

Liliana had done her research. She knew exactly what to say. "I am a refugee. If I return to Cuba, I will be in danger."

"You have come to the right place, Ms. Sánchez." He pointed to a pitcher of water on the desk.

"*Gracias, señor*—thank you, sir."

They both smiled.

Five years, including countless hours of fingernail-biting waiting to hear from the Canadian immigration authorities—and waiting tables—later, Liliana had become a Canadian citizen. She then managed to jump through all the hoops required by the Canadian government until once again she was working at her chosen profession. Loans had been taken out and repaid, but the one loan that could never be repaid was Edward Jones's investment of professional and emotional support.

When she had first arrived in the capital city of St. John's, she had gone to the Association for New Canadians. They had found her lodgings, paid for by the government, but more importantly, they had introduced her to Dr. Jones through a hosting program. Dr. Jones and his wife, Dr. Nicole Cumberland, taught at the university, medicine, and classics respectively.

They had become fast friends almost immediately, and remained close until Edward's death and Nicole's subsequent move to Australia to be with her daughter and her grandchildren. Liliana's background in pharmacology had fascinated Edward; he had been especially intrigued by how the Cubans dealt with pain. During their friendship, Edward had become part of a movement to define pain as the fifth vital sign, which, like temperature and blood pressure, must be managed without concession. It was during this time that the drug hydrocodone stepped into the spotlight. It was the perfect fix—or so it seemed.

In Cuba, pain management was treated differently: tolerable pain levels were seen as a necessity and pain management was a broad equation of chemical, spiritual, holistic and diversionary methods. This had intrigued Edward, that and Liliana's sharp intellect. Her association with him had helped her professionally, although she would have arrived at the university on her own eventually. What he and his wife had given her at that terrible long-ago time, when her soul was split between Cuba and her new-found land, was a place of peace and belonging.

The East Coast Trail followed the shoreline for over three hundred kilometres south, all the way to Cappahayden. Luke was struggling with the first two hundred metres. But then the first two hundred meters were straight up a path that looked more like a rock slide.

Angéline was already at the top of the path, waiting beside an old gun battery for Luke to catch up. She picked a single leaf of mint and rubbed it between her fingers. The wind was busy in the trees, making the last few dead leaves shiver. A sparrow swooped across the path in front of her. She took a deep breath and looked up at the sky: it was intensely blue. A gull soared overhead. It reminded Angéline of the white egret above Magnolia Bridge. Her dreams felt so real, sometimes more real than her days. She thought about her desire to go home. Right now though, she was happy where she stood. She reached her arms towards the sky and the gull.

Luke was at the top of the hill now; his back was beginning to hurt. There she was, standing at the edge of the gun battery with her arms outstretched like a sun worshipper. The only thing he'd worship right now was a cold beer. He loved nature too—after all, that used to be his job, writing for a nature magazine—but at the moment the environment was killing him.

Angéline dropped her arms. "Isn't this beautiful, Luke?"

"Beautiful? I've got an idea, let's walk, no run, all the friggin' way to Cappahayden."

"Luke!"

"My back."

"Sorry. You okay?"

"Not really. When you said a walk, I thought a road, not a damn mountain."

"I'm so sorry, it's just that I've heard about this place and wanted to have a look."

"Okay, have a good look right now before we head home."

"Fair enough."

There wasn't much left of the old gun battery and what was left was covered with foliage. And graffiti: "Are you living in the real world?" What the hell was that supposed to mean, real world? Was there another world, a world beyond the one that stared him in the face every day? The one that brought him pain. And pleasure. Sometimes he did sense other worlds, particularly after his morning dose of oxy. He wished he had his pills right now. It felt as though a razor blade had lodged in his back. Other than when he pushed himself to extremes, like on the walk today, the pain had all but disappeared.

He always had a few extra pills around; his prescription said take when needed. At the end of the month, sometimes more than a dozen pills were left in the bottle. Since he'd met Caleb, though, extras were slim. Caleb didn't have a drug plan, not a legitimate one, anyway, so Luke helped him out. He knew it was illegal, but sometimes the law was short-sighted, and he liked the old guy.

As Angéline and Luke made their way back down the hill towards Fort Amherst, an opening appeared in the woods. It gave on to a wild vista, rugged cliffs and ragged forest and a cradled harbour, its contents rocking gently in the wind. Not much was cultivated here; so much granite, so little soil. Luke couldn't see the people in the city on the other side, but he knew they were there somewhere, making money to feed their kids and their habits. And addictions.

Luke put his arms around Angéline, kissed her lips. "I love you, my darling."

"I love you, Luke."

"Honey, I need to ask you something."

Conversation was always easy between the two of them, but whenever Luke was ready to ask something serious, he always prefaced it with, "Honey, I need to ask you something." Angéline prepared herself. She admired his honesty but sometimes she feared it. She took his hands in hers.

"What is it, what's on your mind?"

"You know that meeting, the one with Dr. Sánchez?"

"I've been wondering."

"Well, I was going to tell you yesterday."

"I know; I just wasn't up to a serious conversation about anything yesterday. But I'm all ears now, go ahead."

"Dr. Sánchez—Liliana—is working on something she thinks can help me. Something that she worked on as a student in Cuba—before she defected."

"Why does she want to help you?"

"Apparently, I fit some kind of profile. She wants me as a guinea pig."

"So, who is she anyway?"

"She's a pharmacy professor, works at the university. She's Cuban, defected in Gander at the start of the Special Period, which was in the early nineties when almost all supplies coming into Cuba from Russia dried up because of the breakup of the Soviet Union.

"Liliana had a Russian partner, and they were working on finding something that would cure drug addiction. Cuba was part of the Colombian traffic route and Afghanistan was feeding heroin to its Russian neighbours."

"But what's this got to do with you?"

"Well, Liliana lost contact with her Russian partner just when the two of them were on the cusp of a breakthrough. She says their discovery would have been worth billions. Apparently, Dr. Kolosov made one last trip to Havana, but Liliana had already defected. She figures he's dead, probably murdered by some Russian oligarch who's making millions off the sale of heroin. She's tried and tried to get in touch with him, but he seems to have disappeared without a trace."

"Jesus, Luke. This is nuts. I can't . . ."

Luke raised his hand, his palm facing her. "Hear me out. Towards the end, both Liliana and Kolosov got worried. They figured out that the drug tzars were controlling the governments. So, medicine that would eliminate addiction was the last thing those in power wanted. Liliana and Kolosov thought their lives were in danger, and she decided to get out of Cuba while she could. On one of her trips to Moscow, she defected in Gander. She moved to St. John's and several years later received a package in the mail—the formula."

Angéline made a face and folded her arms over her chest. "She must be really hot, Luke, otherwise there's no way you'd believe a word of this. You don't really believe it, do you?"

"She's well into her fifties, Angéline. But, yeah, there is something attractive about her—she's going to pay twenty thousand dollars cash if I agree to the trial. Twenty thousand. Imagine what we could do with twenty grand."

"Nice, but not worth a dead partner. I think you're out of your mind. But I'll sleep on it."

12

Pedro clenched his teeth and waited for the phone to stop ringing, but it didn't. Every morning after a big win the state-run radio station wanted to get his story. There was nothing like a baseball hero to prop up a tired system. Not that he cared about the system, he just wanted to play ball. No matter what part you played, it was all about the team and the win. And the fans. And there was something about the beaten leather and pungent smell of a baseball glove . . . and the ball, the beautiful ball, was as close to perfection as anything he knew. Each scarlet stitch was like a scar on a woman's back, and he loved to run his hand over them. He picked up the baseball by the bed and threatened the phone with it. But, as usual, the phone won. He got up and answered it.

"*Hola.*"

"*Hola,* Pedro?"

The voice was simmering with emotion.

"Pedro—*es esta* Pedro Cienfuegos?"

"*Sí,* Pedro Cienfuegos.*"

"Pedro, *esta es* Liliana—Liliana Sánchez."

Memories shot across his mind. She had left when he was twelve—and not a word since. She had been the closest thing to a mother he'd had.

"Liliana! *Where* are you?"

"In Canada. Newfoundland."

"It's been so long, Liliana. Good to hear your voice." He felt tears coming into his own voice and cleared his throat. "I still have the baseball, Liliana—it's here. In my hand."

"Oh, Pedro, if only we could throw that ball again. You and me, like old times. I hear you throw the ball fast these days. They call you Ciento, *sí*?"

"Yes, but I would go easy on you. Why didn't you call me before, why are you calling me now, Liliana?"

"I never called before because the CDR would be monitoring and for you to be caught speaking with a deserter would put you in harm's way. But things are changing, yes?"

Pedro knew that almost everyone in Cuba was monitored. No one was safe from the eyes and ears of the state. And those who thought they were free were often the ones most watched. Even the bread man had eyes and ears. Just speaking the wrong word could be trouble. No one was above the state's paranoia, no one.

"Yes, things are changing, but slowly."

"So, you must come here. To Newfoundland. You are forty; soon, you will mean nothing to them. What then? I can help you, Pedro."

The line went dead. The phone lines were like the cars—old and held together with whatever you could scrounge.

"Hello? Liliana, are you there?" There was no response, only the buzz of a dead line. For years, Pedro had hoped Liliana would contact him, and now she had. But what did it mean, really, except a pang in his heart for the days of his childhood? He hung up the receiver and went back to bed. A knock sounded at his door. He was used to the frequent knocks, mostly local kids wanting an autograph. Sometimes he'd walk up the street to the crossroads, where the kids played, and give a pitching lesson.

He opened the door. It wasn't a kid, it was his father with his arms extended, wearing a smile like the rising sun. A white *guayabera* hung gracefully on him,

making him look official and relaxed at the same time.
Pedro wondered which hat he was wearing—the
father's or the politburo member's?

"*Buenos días,* Papa."

"*Felicidades,* Pedro."

"*Muchas gracias,* Papa."

"You still throw fast, Pedro."

"*Sí,* Papa, but I'm forty."

"That is why I am here, Pedro, to thank you
on behalf of the party. You have made your
countrymen proud. Raúl would like you to take a
position with the National Institute of Sport. This is
my happiest moment, Pedro. I'm an old man, it's fifty-
six years since the revolution."

"You have made your countrymen proud."
Pedro replayed the words in his head. Since he was
born, more than half a million of his countrymen had
escaped the island. Because they were *proud?*

"Well . . . I am not sure what to say, Papa."

"This is your reward, Pedro. You are set for
life. You need only to accept."

Pedro had never crossed his father. He knew
what the outcome would be: the state always loomed

large behind the father figure. But Pedro was older now, and wiser. And while baseball, booze and women had been his life, a longing for freedom—of speech, thought, movement—lingered deep within him.

"Have you seen the people, Papa? Not the privileged ones like you."

"Pedro, how dare you! Have you forgotten our history? Our fight?"

"It's not that, Papa. We must own up: the experiment has failed. Look closely at our country and its people. Both dying of neglect, only basic survival in their future. What kind of life is that? What about freedom, Papa? Tyranny is still tyranny, no matter the politics."

"If you were not my son, I would report you."

"For what, Papa, for what?"

"For speaking against the state. So many fought to give you a good life. And the state has sheltered you from yourself, you and your wild ways. What have I done to deserve this betrayal?"

"Papa, it's not you, it's the system. A system that needs help. Our leaders beat down the very people they purport to help. And you, like them, are brainwashed. Too entrenched in your mind to see through your eyes. You need to see from the outside, as I have. I do not want the job; it is only propaganda. Ciento and Raúl, I can see it on the front page of the *Granma*. I will continue to play baseball for my country as long as I can. As the bread man said just this morning, I give hope to my countrymen. If that is all I do, I have done my work."

"This is impossible, Pedro. You need to think this over. It could be dangerous."

"See, Papa, this is what I mean."

"Pedro, my son, you will call me tomorrow with the right answer, yes?"

"We must do what is right for ourselves, Papa. Your right and my right are different."

Pedro thought about mentioning the call that he had received from Liliana. His father had loved her; she had taken great care of his wife during her illness. And she had tended to young Pedro's every need. It was the death of Pedro's mother that had inspired Liliana to work in pharmacology. She had wondered about the drugs that were being fed to her aunt. But mostly she was inspired by her aunt's power of belief. In the end, Pedro's mother had stopped all her medications and honoured only the religion that she worshipped—Santería. The Santería orisha of healing, divination and wisdom was Orula. Pedro's mother had prayed to Orula for a longer life, in the hopes of seeing her son pitch his first game. And despite a prognosis of only two months, she lived for another three years, long enough to see Pedro throw. She had fought her battles from within and left her mortality in the hands of belief, not medicine. Pedro's mother had been gone for almost thirty years and Liliana about the same. Both free, now. In different ways.

"Papa . . . ah, forget it."

"What, Pedro?"

Sometimes things were best left unsaid. Turning down an offer from the Politburo was one thing, speaking against the revolution was quite another. Conversing with the unfaithful was pure sedition.

"I have done my work, Pedro. Yes is the only answer I will accept. I love you, son."

13

Inspector Myrick lined up three pills on his desk. The pink one inscribed K56 was scarce these days. Doctors called it oxycodone hydrochloride. Pushers called it hillbilly heroin. Mostly it was just called oxy. Myrick chuckled at the info sheet, which stated that habit-forming was a side effect. He wondered when addiction had morphed into some pussy euphemism like "habit-forming." Watching TV was habit forming, taking oxy was pure fucking hell.

Pill number two—round and white, stamped OC 80—was OxyContin, a so-called tamper-proof version of oxycodone that was released slowly into the bloodstream.

But on the street, "tamper-proof" wasn't a deterrent, it was a challenge, and an easy challenge at that: all you had to do was scrape off the coating, crush the pill into a powder and snort, smoke or inject the stuff. And then you got the big bonus, a twelve-hour dosage all at once. If you survived it, life would be really good. For a few hours, anyway. Then nothing but a scramble for the next hit and a dope-sickness that would have you puking your guts up or scratching the phantom itch off your face. Big Pharma had pushed hundreds of tons of OxyContin and pocketed over a billion dollars per year. A fine of more than six hundred million dollars for fraudulent advertising hadn't slowed them down a bit.

Pill number three, the one he got from Caleb Buckle, was pink also, with ON on one side and 80 on the other: OxyNEO, Big Pharma's latest morphine analgesic. It was impossible to break down. Well, not impossible, but almost. But now there was fentanyl. He didn't even want to think about that.

Myrick pushed back his office chair and tossed his feet onto the desk. His hands were already clasped behind his head. There wasn't any fanfare, just a moment of lucidity. And a nod to his few accomplishments. Still, though, he wondered how much longer he could stay on the job. He closed his eyes and pleaded for nothingness, a complete blank. But blanks must be only for the dead. Because if it wasn't the present playing in his head, it was the future. Or the goddamned past.

Whenever the past turned up, one face was always there, that of his long-time police partner, Frank Casey. Their partnership had ended after a drug bust went bad. Myrick had been shot in the arm and Casey had been dragged along for a half mile with his arm wedged in the window of a getaway car. Casey's spinal injuries had confined him to a wheelchair. Myrick couldn't shake that night from his head, or the guilt he felt about not having been able to save Casey from the half-life he lived now. But there was one thing he could do, and he did it. He could ease Casey's pain and his own.

His old partner was in constant pain, and had built up a tolerance to opiates. Only high doses worked for him now, but his doctor wouldn't prescribe them. And there was no way Casey could gain access to street dealers, not in a wheelchair in this city.

"Noble cause corruption" was what the lawyers called it when someone broke the law because of their ethics, their desire to help someone. In Myrick's opinion, the only corruption in his old partner's case was the evil that had put him in a wheelchair. Myrick knew a guy who could help Casey, a blind homeless man named Caleb Buckle.

The office phone rang, and he picked it up. It was Myrick's receptionist. "Ms. Stapleton is here."

"Oh Jesus, Miss Congeniality. Send her in, I s'pose."

It had been just over a year since Carol Stapleton had taken a job with the force. Degrees in criminology and social work made her the perfect candidate to advise fellow officers on how to handle the homeless and the addicted.

Carol opened the door and entered Myrick's office. Myrick looked up reluctantly from the file open on his desk.

"Ah, Carol, nice to see you. Always a pleasure when the *caring* side of the department stops by."

"Sarcasm, Inspector? We haven't even started yet. You don't even know why I'm here."

"I know why and before you begin, let me just say that every single day my officers do the best they can. They're not social workers, they're cops."

"Maybe I should leave and come back later."

"It's never a good time, Carol, but, what the hell—go ahead, have your say."

"Addiction is a disease, Inspector. We need to treat addicts with dignity, care and understanding. What part of that do you have difficulty with?"

"How about all of it? Addicts are the bad guys and we're the good guys. What part of that do you have difficulty with? If addicts break the law, we arrest them. Isn't that the way it works? Or am I missing something? One more thing: addicts are usually whacked out of their goddamn trees—you never know what they're going to do. And in case you don't know, cops aren't their favourite people. And it's bullshit like this that makes their job even more difficult."

"All I'm saying, Inspector, you treat addicts with compassion and you'll do a better job of your job."

"Someone give you a lifetime pass for Disneyland, Ms. Stapleton?"

"Smartass comments don't help, Inspector. Addiction is a disease and we need to be aware of the suffering. That's all."

"No, Carol, you're wrong, addiction is a symptom, a symptom of a disease called misery. That's what it is. And a fix is the only escape. And, for the love of God, don't get in the way because there ain't no rules. Ever tried playing with no rules, Carol? Cops are all about rules, addicts don't give a fuck. How fair is that? And for the record, I know first-hand about addiction, I've got my own problems—mostly caused by crap like this."

"I'm sorry about that, Myrick." Carol Stapleton pushed her glasses onto the top of her head and sighed. Myrick was due to retire soon. She wondered where old dinosaurs went. Possibly Jurassic Park. She thought there might actually be a theme park of that name in California. Perhaps they could take up a collection. Most of the force wouldn't be able to get out their wallets fast enough. That thought made her smile for the first time since she'd walked into his office.

"Don't be sorry, Carol, just stay out of the goddamn way. And for the record, the chief already knows about my problems. No need to go shooting your mouth off upstairs."

14

Pedro reached for his yellow and green beads and rubbed them between his fingers. He pulled the beads apart and looked closely at the string; it was worn and ready to break. The beads were a symbol of the orisha Orula, who knew the destiny of every human being. Pedro had honoured Orula since he was seven, with gifts of oil and honey at his hallway shrine. October fourth was Orula's feast day, and four was Pedro's uniform number.

But it wasn't baseball today, it was his other life, the one off the field. The one where the rule book was still being written, the one that never had absolute wins or losses. And the one where averages didn't matter. Because here, on this island, it was about getting by. He was at a crossroads: family, freedom, loyalty and truth were its signposts. Whatever path he chose, there would be an ache that lingered forever— did I do the right thing?

Just a few times in his life had Pedro needed to consult the orisha Elegguá, Elegguá the guardian of doors and the keeper of crossroads. Only Elegguá could guide him through the dirty waters of doubt.

It was a beguiling juxtaposition, the soft white cloth draped over a tall man, the shiny black face and a rusted iron gate. A priest, a santero. He smiled graciously as he welcomed Pedro into his home. A heavy smell of sandalwood and cinnamon filled the little room. A black hen scurried around, stopping once to cock her head and turn a bright eye towards the two men. An elaborate red and black shrine covered an entire wall. In the centre was a large wooden dish containing a small wooden statue of a child. This represented Elegguá. Pedro presented gifts of candy, honey and tobacco to the child in the dish.

Although Pedro believed firmly in it, he had never been to the inner world. He had been close: on the mound of Estadio Latinoamericano the swell of the mystical would sometimes wash over him. Fingering the green and yellow necklace, all he could see was the ball and home plate. The fans were invisible, and they screamed silently.

The santero tossed twenty-one cowrie shells onto a board, each one landing as the gods divined, as they'd done for thousands of years. The priest was in a trans-like state, mumbling and shaking. One of his hands faced upwards and his eyes had a beseeching look in them.

"Pedro, Pedro Cienfuegos, the shells have spoken."

Twenty-one shells lay on the board, their porcelain-like surfaces glinting in the light that cut a perfect line through the dust. Two shells had landed with the tooth-edged slit facing upwards.

"It is clear, Pedro: you must go. You must leave this island. The path itself is not clear, but there is brightness in the distance. Orula will watch over you."

The santero grabbed the hen, pulled back the black feathers and slit her neck. A fountain of blood poured over the shrine. Pedro was so awash in the glory that for a moment he forgot why he was there. When he turned to leave, he glanced into the kitchen: a crumpled poster was taped to the wall above the kitchen table. His own image looked back at him; underneath was written, in large black letters, "Pedro Cienfuegos, *Ciento el Magnífico*."

Liliana was pulling him one way, his father countering. His beautiful Cuba cradled his soul, but the call of freedom echoed in the distance. Now the orisha had spoken to him, strongly. And there was his face and name on the priest's wall. The name Cienfuegos was not a name that one associated with surrender.

15

When Liliana wasn't working, she was reading, and when she wasn't reading, she volunteered at a methadone clinic. It was just across the lake from her apartment, at the old American armed forces base. The methadone clinic looked like 1943 and smelled like it too. The aluminum siding and muted green walls gave it an air of neglect and uncaring. But every person who worked and volunteered there cared enough for a dozen people. And no one cared more than Liliana Sánchez.

People from every walk of life came to the clinic, hoping to beat their addictions. Trouble was there was no cure-all. Methadone and its sister drugs came with a full sheet of side effects. Methadone was just one opiate replacing another. But then, the opiate shell game was nothing new: a hundred years ago, British missionaries dispensed morphine (Jesus opium) to the Chinese to cure their opium addictions.

Liliana knew that story and every other fabrication that followed: codeine, methadone, hydrocodone, hydromorphone, oxycodone, oxycontin,

OxyNEO, all promised to be non-addictive, but the measure of time always delivered a different story and that story had gone on far too long. Liliana was ready to make her move.

Sometimes she walked up Signal Hill across the North Head trail to Cuckold's Cove and through Quidi Vidi Village before she made her way around the lake to the clinic. What lovely names those were. Liliana had everything she needed, and she loved Newfoundland, but it was a strange place. Gentle yet harsh.

As she walked, she thought about her plan. She had to do it by herself. The university was too public; besides the university brass would never agree to her methods. She knew that running her own trial would be ethically and legally wrong and that it was counter to everything she had learned and everything she taught. But this was about one thing only, the well-being of patients—surely that superseded everything. Money wasn't part of the equation, and while her own ethics might be questionable, those of Big Pharma were contemptible. They spent millions of dollars on sales representatives and advertising. Good medicines shouldn't have to be, figuratively, pushed down people's throats. If they worked, they would sell themselves.

Addiction was big business. But recovery was even bigger, worth over sixty billion dollars a year. Sometimes it was hard to tell the good guys from the bad. Then there were the insurance companies, skimping, throwing money at a thirty-day supply of OxyContin rather than more expensive forms of pain therapy. The American Center for Disease Control had just announced that, in the United States alone, more than one hundred and eighty thousand people had died since 1999 of prescription opioids.

A great tide of deceit had washed over the continent. For Liliana Sánchez, there was no better time. For over a year, she had been following Luke Delaney's fight with opioid addiction. As much as he tried to beat it, he kept falling off the wagon. He was the perfect candidate.

When Liliana's story broke, and it would, she would concoct a story about human trials that happened somewhere in a northern Russian gulag. She imagined the media blitz, everything from "This is the most despicable act of health betrayal in the last fifty years" to "Liliana Sánchez is a medical hero like Banting and Best."

16

The floral smell of saffron moved from the kitchen into the living room, where Luke was watching the evening news. The beer on the table in front of him, Iceberg, made him think of his old bar acquaintance Iceberg. Nobody knew how Iceberg got his name, but it was probably something to do with his theories. He loved to share them, especially when he was drunk, which was nearly always. "Icebergs, see, I'm gonna tell ya, see, fuckin' icebergs, man—they's mo' shit goin' down below the shit line, know what I mean? Icebergs is like life, man—are you hearin' me?"

Luke wondered about what might be going on beneath the surface with Liliana Sánchez. Somehow, though, he trusted her implicitly. Maybe he, Luke Delaney, just happened to be the right person at the right place at the right time. That didn't happen much in life, but when it did you had to jump.

"Dinner's almost ready."

"Coming."

"No, I want to watch the news—you can come and get yours when it's ready and I'll bring mine

out too. They're doing a bit on New Orleans tonight."
Some local tradespeople had gone down to help
rebuild after Katrina and, even after a decade, some
were still going down there. She would have liked to
have gone to New Orleans herself, but she couldn't
face up to the fact that the family home was no longer
there.

Angéline was happy when she was in the
kitchen; it was her favourite room. She loved to cook,
and she loved the evening light that shone through the
west window. Added to the show were the branches of
the backyard maple, shadow dancing on the
cupboards. She felt like dancing with them.

Her weakness, or, as Luke said, her strength,
was the big grocery store with its seemingly limitless
selections. She was particularly fond of food from
foreign lands, like tonight's dinner, kabobs with
saffron rice from Azerbaijan.

If only the dreams would go away. Angéline
had tried talk therapy and dream specialists. Nothing
worked. Then it was pills. "Try this," they'd say. Then
the dizzy spells and nausea would come. "Okay, this is
how we deal with that." And on it went until her pill

case wouldn't snap shut. Appointment after appointment ended with the same refrain, "Before you know it, you'll be back to normal." But the dream remained, and she'd almost forgotten what normal was. Her bedroom, her beautiful refuge, had become the dreaded chamber. The fear of the dream had become as debilitating as the dream itself. She had become a hostage to the night, trying with all her power to keep her eyes from closing.

"Our first story this evening takes us to the west end of St. John's, where there's been another holdup."

"Good evening. Robbers got away with an undisclosed amount of cash from Walsh's Grocery and Confectionery on Hamilton. This is the third time this store has been held up in as many months."

"Wow, Luke. I wonder what's up with that."

"Drugs. It's rampant. Look at me, for Christ's sake. If I couldn't get my fix—might as well call it that—who knows?"

The television image changed. A brass band moved across the screen.

"Frenchman Street! – Look, Luke, I know that spot."

A journalist did her best to talk over the street noise.

"More than a decade has passed since Katrina turned the land to water. They still talked about it here. How could they not? Clearing and rebuilding are everywhere. The emotional recovery has been the hardest, however. That and getting rid of the mud. But time, the great healer, has proven its worth again. New Orleans never gave up: the city and its people are a testament to the power of the human spirit; over which nature's wrath can never prevail. And, leading the parade, there's music, a healer as great as time: zydeco, ragtime, brass band, jazz, Dixieland.

"New Orleans, the Crescent City, the Big Easy: Creoles from France, Spain, Haiti and Cuba, Mardi Gras, gumbo, jambalaya, catfish pie . . ."

Luke turned to Angéline.

"Cuba, New Orleans, you know about that?"

"Sure. My ancestors were Haitian. They went to Cuba to cut cane and from there they moved to

New Orleans. That's where my mother was born, and twenty-three years later she met my father, a Cajun."

"Imagine our child," Luke said jokingly. "Haitian, Cajun, Irish, Armenian. Poor little thing."

"This might be a good time to tell you, Luke."

"What? You kidding me? Really?"

"Noooo, not a baby."

"Jesus, Angéline. Don't do that. What then?"

"Voodoo—my mother. She practised it. Unfortunately, it's gotten a bad name, mostly because of the movies. You know, voodoo dolls and bad spells. Truth is, by pointing a finger at somebody else, you have three pointing back at you. Try it. It's a dangerous thing to wish bad things on another person. It'll come back on you threefold, according to the voodoo way."

"Makes sense, but sounds like you're apologizing. Don't bother. My background isn't exactly stellar. Irish Roman Catholic. Imagine the weight I carry."

"Well, at least the Roman Catholic church has recognized voodoo for its true worth: one more path to God. After all, Louisiana voodoo and Roman Catholicism are deeply enmeshed. As you know,

African slaves were forbidden to practice their religion, so they incorporated it into Christianity. And that wasn't so hard, because the two religions have strong similarities: belief in one God, belief in divine intermediaries, the saints and the lwas. All the same, as I told you, for some reason my father hated voodoo and my mother lived by it. Their beliefs were different, but they loved each other so much. They were each other's every reason for living, emotional, mental, physical. What a love that was. That's what we have—right?" Angéline placed her hand over his.

Luke hadn't assembled all the parts before. But it sounded good. He loved the beauty of her words. But right now, it was her body that spoke the loudest.

"Of course, honey. Of course. That's us."

Luke waited for the embrace that would seal the words. And start the fire.

The next morning Luke and Angéline decided to walk to the old Battery Hotel. The Volvo was acting up, and they wanted time to think and talk before they met with Liliana Sánchez.

It was a fine hike across the downtown, strolling along beside the little shops on Water Street and rambling along the waterfront. A new iron fence prevented them from walking the harbour apron, the place where Luke loved to stroll. It was a grand fence, but it was still a fence. In a way, it reminded him of his addiction, compromising freedom as it did, preventing him from living his life to the fullest.

Luke looked back at the dry dock where welding sparks were flying from the hull of an old ferry boat.

"Everything breaks down, Angel. Guess, that's where we are today. It's never a matter of *if*, it's always a matter of *when*. It's how you respond, that's the real measure. That's what my father used to say."

"Fair enough. I'll try to keep an open mind."

"I'm not big on this either, but up against my addiction, I'll try whatever. And I believe in Liliana."

"An open mind is all I can offer, Luke."

Angéline hooked her arm into Luke's and they made their way towards Signal Hill.

The old Battery Hotel, now Memorial University's Battery Facility, had had a facelift, but it still looked like a spaceship, out of place in the wooden city but still part of it.

Luke and Angéline entered the building and walked down a long hall to Liliana's office. The door was open; they could see Liliana sitting at her desk. Luke knocked lightly, and she looked up.

"Luke, please come in. So happy to see you. And you must be Angéline—such a pleasure."

"Nice to meet you, too."

"Please sit down; can I get you anything? Cup of tea, a Coke?"

Luke shook his head. "No, thank you." Angéline was checking out the place, especially the degrees hanging on the wall.

Liliana noticed Angéline's muted survey of her office. She smiled at Angéline, and said, "There are other diplomas, back in Cuba. I couldn't take everything."

"I understand. So, what else did you study?"

"Mainly pharmacology, but also naturopathic medicines."

"An odd combination, naturopathic and pharmacological?"

"Not really. They are complementary."

Luke looked at Angéline and squinted. She made a face at him and moved towards a chair.

Liliana got up and closed the door. "Let's sit down and discuss why we're here.

"First, thank you both for coming. I do hope you will agree to be a part of this project. On the surface, it may appear that my methods are questionable, but you must understand that it is either my way or Big Pharma's way. And, as you are aware, whenever money is a variable, morality becomes skewed. I'm not in this for money, I have enough money. I'm only interested in the welfare of the sick. Everything is ready, all I need is Luke's cooperation to prove that this will work. And if it does work, and I'm sure it will, there will be bigger trials."

Luke thought he should jump in before Angéline started picking at the cracks. He was too late.

"With all due respect, Dr. Sánchez, unethical is one thing, but what about dangerous?"

"I understand your concerns; however, you have to believe me, there is no danger in my methods. As I said I don't care about the money; I have enough to live comfortably on. And why would a person want more than enough? I lived in Havana at the beginning of the Special Period, when there was never enough. I know what it's like to be without food and to be unwell. I have the ways and means to help you, Luke, but I also need you to help me. Luke, you deserve better: an addiction to opiates is not your fault. Your quality of life has been diminished, and I'm here to help you return to the old Luke Delaney. I know you want to; you've tried everything, and nothing has worked for you: I can't give you specifics about the treatment until you've decided to commit. The only thing I can say is there will be no pain involved in the treatment. A daily pill, with absolutely no side effects. I'm sure you and Angéline will want to discuss this, so there is no need to make a decision today, but I will need to know within a week."

"For some strange reason, I've known from our first meeting that I want to be in on this. And despite your methods, I trust you." Luke had a loopy grin on his face, which seemed to indicate relief and optimism.

It was evident from the confused look on Angéline's face that she wasn't ready for a wholesale commitment, but neither was she about to eat Liliana alive or walk out.

"Let me put it this way: I trust Luke. And clearly, he trusts you. So, despite everything that's wrong with this, I guess I'm in. And one other thing: if anything goes wrong, we can get out whenever we want. Right?"

"Of course, you can. And you can keep the money."

For a moment, they had forgotten about the money. Liliana reached into a desk drawer, pulled out a large envelope of cash and handed it across the desk to Luke.

"As promised, your payment for taking part in this project. But please don't deposit the whole amount at one time. Sometimes banks are suspicious of large cash deposits."

"So, when do we start, Liliana?"

"I'll call you in a few days."

"Thank you, Liliana, thank you very much."

"Yes, thank you, Liliana. I look forward to meeting you again." Angéline's words seemed remote to her. Far from her mouth, close to her gut, she felt like she had just sold her soul.

"Oh yes and one other thing: no one must know about this trial, no one. If the university were to find out, at the very least I would be fired. But I'm willing to risk all for the sake of your wellness. And later, the wellness of hundreds of thousands of others."

17

Pedro didn't sleep well. He tossed and turned, and when he finally dozed off, the tossing continued. The night was playing out the previous day. For a moment, he thought about drawing two columns: reasons to stay and reasons to leave, but then this wasn't about objectivity, it was about living, and life's decisions came from the gut. "Use your intuition" was a refrain he had heard from his father, but then that was part of the problem: his gut was telling him to leave. He was half awake when he heard the old man with the crumpled leather face outside the window, blowing his whistle and repeating the old refrain.

"Pan y mantequilla! Paan y mantequilla, Pann y mantequilla!"

A knock on his door followed.

Pedro answered the door. "Old man, you are the one thing I can count on."

"Ahh, Ciento, the whole country counts on you, I am only the bread man."

"Thank you, old man. You are too kind. One loaf, please."

"Ciento, here is a letter. You were away, yesterday, yes?"

"Yes, old man, I was away. Who is the letter from?"

"I don't know, a man passed me on the street and said it was for you. That's all I know. My sight is bad; he sounded Cuban, but smelled like a *gringo*."

"A *gringo*, what do they smell like, old man?" Pedro said with a grin.

"Like money."

"And what's the smell of money, old man?"

"Like *gringo*."

"You are funny, old man. Thank you."

"You are welcome, Ciento. Tomorrow?"

"Of course."

Pedro turned and walked towards his chair. He sat down. With great care, he tore the end of the envelope and pulled out the letter. The paper was white with watermarks. If it were Cuban, it would have been newsprint. The message was handwritten and short: "Yellow dress, Dos Hermanos. Wednesday, November 16, 10:00 a.m."

It wasn't unusual that women wanted to meet up with him, but this had the ring of something different. Something special. And then, for a moment, he thought the worst. Maybe the CDR wanted to have a word with him. He looked at his watch: it was 9:00 a.m. The date read Wednesday, November 16. He only had one hour to get ready. His Orula beads were always the first to go on, but they looked more tattered than ever, kept intact by one worn yellow thread. If the string broke, it could only mean one thing.

A mix of thrill and anxiety hit Pedro as he opened the door to the oldest bar in Havana, Dos Hermanos. It was the same feeling he got when he stepped on the mound of Latinoamericano. But here the smell of rum and fresh-pummelled mint hung in the air. In Havana, *mojitos,* rum cocktails, were more prominent than the sun. They started before dawn and went well after dark.

Dos Hermanos was by the harbour. Once a seedy bar for the locals, it had become the go-to place for tourists. The essence of Hemingway, Lorca and Brando still hung in the ether. And the tourists were everywhere, thicker than ever before. There were Yanks, the ones who only a year ago were the dreaded enemy. Now they were new best friends, with their flowery shirts and designer sunglasses, and, as the old man said, the smell of money.

Trying his best to conceal his identity, Pedro pulled his cap down over his eyes. But at the bar it was mostly tourists; no one would recognize him. None of the locals could afford to drink in this place, not now anyway. And the few bartenders who knew him were too busy pouring rum to notice the great Ciento. He looked around for the woman with the yellow dress. And there she was, in the corner, underneath a picture of Federico Garcia Lorca. She was facing in the opposite direction. He walked over and touched her on the back. She turned around.

"Pedro, Pedro Cienfuegos! So nice to finally meet you. I'm Lily Collingwood from Boston. I am happy that you have decided to come. Please sit down."

"Nice to meet you, Señorita Collingwood."

"Please call me Lily."

"If you wish. Why have you come to Havana, Lily?"

"We need to get right down to it. We shouldn't be seen."

"*Sí.*"

"I would like you to come to Boston and play for the Red Sox."

Pedro thought that his eyes and ears were playing tricks. He looked over his shoulder for Elegguá. You never knew when the trickster was about.

"This must be some kind of joke."

"No, Pedro, this is not a joke, you heard me right. The Boston Red Sox. We like the way you pitch. And we need a closer."

"But, I am forty and at the end of my career. Why would you want me?"

"We've been following you, Pedro—Ciento. We know you throw only a few pitches, but you throw straighter and faster than anyone we've seen."

"I don't know what to say. This is a shock. A chance to play with the Boston Red Sox, the team of Ruth and Williams, Yastrzemski—this is too good to be true. I think I need time."

"This needs to happen quickly, Pedro."

An image played in Pedro's head, a boy wearing a Red Sox hat throwing a baseball to a woman. It was he and Liliana. Then out of the dry, hot air, the sound of Havana street minstrels brought him back to where he was.

"Your job, Lily, what is it?"

"Believe me, signing contracts is not what I usually do. I'm a statistician, but the Red Sox didn't want to raise suspicion, so they sent me. I guess I look like just another tourist."

Pedro took a closer look. While he had had his share of beautiful women, Lily was in a different league. Her ruby lipstick matched her light American skin and emerald eyes. The yellow dress topped it off—it seemed to breathe with her.

"Just another American tourist?" He smiled.

Lily smiled back. "I understand that your country is not very happy about losing its baseball stars, but I have a job to do, and I've come with an offer that will undoubtedly make a better life for you. Maybe this will help you make a decision."

Lily reached into her purse and pulled out a cheque.

"Interested, Pedro?"

He had dreamed of playing in the big leagues, and now the reality stared him in the face. But he could barely understand. Forty, and playing for the Sox?

"You've proven you still have it. Please accept our offer."

Maybe the santero had spoken the truth. It was time for him to leave. Forty and playing for the Sox. Four was his lucky number, maybe forty would be a new beginning. Four always brought something good with it. The only time he stayed away from four was when it came to a walk: four balls. He always pitched strikes; he knew the edges of home plate better than the umpires. And that's all the Red Sox wanted. Pedro looked at the cheque made out to him. The amount was beyond his comprehension. He had to ask Lily what the number was.

"Yes, Pedro, four hundred thousand American dollars. Not pesos."

"More than I get now, which is twenty-eight dollars a month." He smiled. "I accept your offer."

Walking home, the cheque burning a hole in his wallet, Pedro decided to tell no one. Not even the old bread man. The gates to America were open, but the CDR still watched from the shadows.

18

For Caleb, having the police in his back pocket made things easier. Or so he thought. But if things started to unravel, he would end up taking the fall. He worried what might happen to Blackjack.

So, kicking his addiction was the first step in starting a new life. But he would continue to sell, and with any luck, by December he'd be free from using and selling altogether, and be settled in his own room with enough money to get through the winter. At least that was his plan. And his dream. Watching hockey and baseball in a decent place of his own and jumping up and down and howling with Blackjack at the TV was as good as it could get.

Luke turned off Water Street into a side alley where modern brick and ancient stone existed together. The city had been squabbling about the downtown, some pushing progress, others the past. But this was the oldest city in North America and that alone was worth more than all the oil in the sea. History would always be there, you just had to preserve it. Scars from the oil boom were leaving their mark on the landscape and on the seafloor. And worse yet, on the people. Living the high life was great until it was gone. And then dreams turned into nightmares.

"Luke, that you? What are you doing round here—in the middle of the day?"

"I've got something for you."

"What?"

"A bag of pills—want you to have them. I don't need them anymore."

"What, going cold turkey?"

"Kinda."

"Why me?"

"Because I'd like to help you. That's all. Besides, it's either that or toss them. No need to tell me what you're doing with the pills, but no kids. Okay?"

"Yeah, of course. You know me, I'd slit the throat of anyone who sold to kids."

"Yeah. I had to say it, that's all. You know."

"Jesus, Luke, I don't know what to say."

"You're a good man, Caleb. Wish I could help more. I'll be by later on."

"Thanks."

When Luke had gone, Caleb sat down and opened the bag. He reached in: there was more than a handful of pills. He rubbed his finger over the surface of each tablet, ON inscribed one side, 80 on the other. Lately, he'd been able to get a dollar per milligram.

"Blackjack, forty times eighty. You know what that means."

19

At least when Carol Stapleton's heart bled it always bled from the same place; politicians bled from everywhere, mostly their asses. Which happened to be the same place from where they spoke, at least that's how Myrick saw it. He had little time for bullshit. What really pissed him off was that the force had lost the public's respect. There were a few bad apples, and shit happened, but, as far as Myrick was concerned, the RNC was as good as any other force. The day-to-day on the street was like being at war. It wasn't the bruises on the bodies of his officers that worried Myrick, it was the bruises on their minds.

The phone rang, and Myrick groped among the folders, papers and empty coffee mugs on his desk for it.

"Myrick."

"Sir, a Mr. William Saunders from Justice is here to see you."

"Does he have an appointment?"

"No, Inspector."

"For Christ's sake, send him in. But tell him I'm busy, only have ten minutes."

"Sir?"

Just in case he needed it, Myrick pulled out his copy of the *Criminal Code*. It looked like a Bible, and for him it was. His whole life revolved around it. And he followed it to the letter. It was the only thing that made a grain of sense. But politicians like to mince words and sometimes you needed to lay down the law—in a very literal way.

There was a knock on his door. Myrick got up and pasted on his best smile. He didn't like to play games, but he could. To a point.

Myrick opened the door. "Nice to meet you, Mr. Saunders. Please come in and sit down. Coffee?"

"Jesus, no. All I need is something else to wind me up. What the fuck is this Fentanyl crap?"

Myrick had never met Saunders, the assistant deputy minister of Justice, but he already liked the guy. They spoke the same language. "A goddamn problem, that's what it is."

"What the fuck is this stuff?"

Myrick reached into his drawer and hauled out a small bag of pills. He handed it to Saunders.

"In pill form, which is what I just handed to you, it's called the green monster, or fake Oxy, because the pills look like OxyContin 80s right down to the stamps. The powder is called China white. It's a man-made opiate, up to one hundred times more potent than morphine. One kilogram is worth about twenty-one thousand dollars and that same kilogram can be used to make a million tablets. The street value of a tablet is between ten and fifty dollars. Do the math—a goddamn gold mine."

Myrick took a deep breath.

"What's worse, you never know what you're getting. You might think you're getting Oxy, but maybe it's cut with Fentanyl. Next thing you know you've stopped breathing. That's the last thing you'll ever know.

"Then there are the so-called tamper-proof Fentanyl patches. Tamper-proof, baloney; within weeks the street figured how to break that shit down.

"I can give you some local stories, but you might have to pop one of those pills to get through it.

Which would be pure goddamn bliss. Trouble is you may want to do it again. And again.

"By the way, the situation here is not too bad ---yet. But in the west and down south in the land of the free, it's a full-fledged epidemic. We might be an island, but that won't keep the dope out for long, it never has."

"How are we dealing with it, Myrick?"

"Fortunately, we can prevent a few ODs with a shot of naloxone, but that's hardly a fix. By the way, naloxone is made by the same companies that make fentanyl. Creative bastards, yeah? Cash from both sides. You need to fix this, the top of the food chain is where you start."

"I get it, Myrick, but you know as well as I do we don't have the resources to do that, so let's at least deal with the optics. People don't want to see or even hear about this shit. It makes everyone look bad. Cops too."

"So, what you're saying is you can't do nothing at the top, and it's up to cops to clean up this mess. So, why'd you come here?"

"Well done, Myrick. You answered your own question. Every junkie on the street with twenty or more pills—lock 'em up. Because you know as well as I do, they're dealing. The Crown will take care of the rest. And let the media know."

Saunders picked up Myrick's copy of the *Criminal Code* and started flipping pages.

"Right here, Myrick. Part 7.1(1) Controlled Drugs and Substances Act. Possession, for use in the production of or trafficking in substance.

"I'll be in touch."

Just as Saunders shook Myrick's hand and left the office, the phone rang.

Mrs. Andrea Casey is on the line. Shall I put her through?"

"Sure."

"Myrick here. What's up, Andrea?"

"You sitting down? I have bad news."

The tone of Andrea's voice said it all.

"Oh, Jesus. No."

"Frank was in the garage when I found him, slumped over in his wheelchair, with the car running."

"Oh, Jesus."

20

José Martí International Airport was full of American tourists. Compared to the Cuban peso, the Yankee dollar was worth a fortune, and between cigars and rum and hookers, the Caribbean island was as good as getaways got. The wait had been more than fifty years, and, seemingly overnight, the American nightmare had morphed into a new American dream. Although it looked as if the new US president was about to bring it to an end.

Pedro wondered if paradise was always on the other side or did it just appear that way. For a moment, he stood still and looked around at the tourists and thought about his decision. It was a short thought; a moment later he began moving towards the security line. He had told nobody about his departure, not even his father—especially not his father. Leaving Cuba wasn't a big deal anymore, but to avoid suspicion he had purchased a return ticket for the following week.

Compared to those who had braved the Florida Straits before him, his exit would be easy; in some ways, it felt more like a failure than an act of courage.

Pedro approached the security guard at the end of the security line. The guard took a second look at the man with the straw hat pulled down over his eyes.

"Pedro, Pedro Cienfuegos! Your autograph for my boy? Please."

"Of course."

Within seconds a dozen or so airport staff members were trying to shake the hand of their national hero.

"You going to play for the Red Sox, Ciento?" a guard said.

Pedro's heart stopped for a moment. But the accompanying laughter identified it as friendly banter. Pedro responded, in the same joking tone, "*Sí*, I am their new closer." Everyone laughed at the absurdity.

Pedro pulled two baseballs from his backpack and tossed them to the security guards on the other side of the X-ray machine. The guards couldn't believe their good fortune.

Pedro passed through the machine.

"Please sign our baseballs, Ciento," said one of the guards."

Pedro reached for one of the baseballs. "Oh. Sorry, this is my baseball; I have given you the wrong one."

Pedro reached into the bag on the conveyor belt beside him. "Please take this one, it's brand new."

"*Claro,* Ciento, of course."

Pedro placed the old ball, Liliana's ball, back into his bag and turned around and waved to the collection of admiring fans, who waved back. Even an American waved. The American had no idea whom he was waving to, but he would soon know. All of America would know.

21

Even if they were dealing, Myrick didn't like arresting street addicts: they had enough problems. But there was nothing like cleaning up the streets to make things look better than they really were. At least that's what Saunders had said. And while Myrick didn't agree, it had the appearance of a solution. And maybe, for a change, his fellow police officers would be seen as the good guys and gals.

Myrick popped a pill into his mouth and washed it down with cold coffee. Then he left his office and went to the briefing room.

"Good morning, children." This was part sarcasm and part endearment. The truth was they were his family.

"What, coffee hasn't kicked in? More life in a dried-up slug. Time to wake up."

They never knew if he was being serious or funny, so they usually erred on the side of caution. There was a shuffle of bodies and chairs as they shifted in their seats.

"Before we get down to business, I want you to take a minute to remember a brother of our police family, Constable Frank Casey, who died yesterday morning. Constable Casey was the finest partner a cop could have."

About twenty seconds later, Myrick lifted his head. He had held back the tears, but he couldn't stop the watery film from glazing over his eyes. He coughed and threw back his shoulders.

"Let's get right to it. The drug problem is getting out of hand—we need to clean things up. Optics—you know what that is, it's what gives us either a good or bad name. Most people don't care about what they can't see, only what they can see. So, let's get out there and make ourselves visible. Let's give the public a story for their ten-second Facebook feed. More importantly, we get the small-timers and through them we can get the head of the snake—some back-room negotiation goes a long way.

"Okay, get out of here and kick some ass. O'Neil, can I see you for a few minutes—in my office."

Myrick tapped his pencil on his desk. The knock came right on time.

"Come in, O'Neil—close the door." Myrick gestured towards a chair. "Sit down."

"Of course, Inspector."

Myrick stood up and walked to the window with his hands behind his back.

"Remember that file from Cuba? You know— the one with you and the hooker. Thought I could bury it, but it's raised its ugly head. Again."

"Jesus Christ, Inspector."

Myrick pulled a letter from his tunic pocket.

"I'd let you read it, O'Neil, but it takes brains to read. And apparently, you don't have any.

"Let's just say that the Policía Nacional are looking for you. It seems that hooker you screwed is leaving a trail of dead men behind her—old fuckers with weak hearts, thick wallets and an appetite for blue pills. You might wish you met the same end, because the Cuban cops want your sorry ass."

"Prostitution isn't a crime, Inspector. Not in Cuba."

"Neither is fucking someone to death, but stealing their money is. When they finally caught up with the bleached bronco, she had seven wallets, yours included. The old fellas were all accounted for, already in the dirt, but you—you disappeared. And they've been looking for you ever since. They want to return your wallet—with the ten grams of coke they found in the zippered pocket. Jesus H. Christ, O'Neil, hookers and drugs. And your ID in your wallet."

Myrick's face was three shades of red. He reached into his pocket, took out a pill and swallowed more cold coffee.

"What have you got to say, O'Neil? Whatever it is, it better be good. And why didn't you tell me about the wallet? I could have covered your ass."

"I don't know what to say, sir."

"Don't know what to say? Well, I do. There are two things I can do with this: bring it to the chief or bring it to the chief."

"Oh, Jesus. That'll finish me. I've got a wife, a kid."

"That really helps. Coke, hooker, wife and kid. And cop. Paint it any way you like, you fucked up and now it's time to pay up. As simple as that."

O'Neil felt like crying, but he wouldn't do that, not in front of Myrick, not with his uniform on. What hurt most, was that he was a good cop. But no one cared about that. Not now, not when the chips were down.

"So, are you going to go to the chief with this, sir?"

O'Neil's face was a study in misery. Myrick had him right where he wanted him—ready to beg for mercy.

22

Freezing rain trickled down Liliana's window. She watched as three droplets moved towards the sill. The droplet she had chosen to win was lagging behind the other two. She hoped it wasn't an omen, not now, not while preparing for what was ahead. Today, it was the theatre of medicine, or *el juego*, the game, and if something went wrong, the experiment was doomed.

Taking care of Pedro's mother was when Liliana first recognized *el juego*. She was nineteen, and had written an entry in her journal about it:

Olivia seems to feel better when she prays at her shrine or when she speaks to her santero. And certain doctors make her feel better. She wants to live long enough to see Pedro play in the minors, and I think her spirit is strong enough for this to happen, although the doctors say otherwise.

It was at that time that Liliana started to believe that there was more to medicine than pharmaceuticals. She enrolled in at the University of Medical Sciences of Havana, but she also explored Eastern medicine, hypnotism, chi, acupuncture and homeopathy. The Eastern approach to healing fascinated her. In the East, the fundamentals never changed, only the interpretation of them, whereas the Western approach was a straight line always moving forward, with little honouring of the past.

She also took an interest in people who had a proclivity for the extraordinary, like Franz Mesmer, an eighteenth-century German physician who used magnets to cure disease. Along with the magnets draped from his silk and leather jacket, he used theatre and music. Mesmer was convincing, intelligent and charismatic. Thousands were healed of their maladies, and Mesmer became the talk of the day, with the likes of Amadeus Mozart singing his praises. But Mesmer realized eventually that the healing was a result of the power of suggestion, which was why he was known as the father of hypnotism—or mesmerism. Call it what you like, it worked.

The third droplet reached the window sill.

The phone rang; Liliana picked it up.

"Hello."

"Yes, hello, Dr. Sánchez, please."

"Yes, this is Dr. Sánchez."

"Dr. Sánchez, this is Lily Collingwood with
the Boston Red Sox."

"Boston Red Sox, the baseball team? Are you
sure you have the right number?"

"I think so, if this is Dr. Liliana Sánchez in St.
John's, Newfoundland."

The woman pronounced it "New Funlund,"
which made Liliana smile. "Well, that's me, but the
Boston Red Sox?"

"I'm calling on behalf of Pedro Cienfuegos.
You know Pedro?"

"Yes, I know Pedro, I took care of him as a
boy. And we talked not long ago. Is there a problem?"

"No, no problem. Pedro wanted me to tell
you the news. But hold on, he's right here. He can tell
you himself."

"Liliana, this is Pedro."

"Oh, Pedro—how are you? What's going on?"

"I am well, I'm in Boston, Liliana—the
United States. I've been asked to play for the Red
Sox!"

"What, do I hear you right?—Pedro
Cienfuegos, Pedro Juan Cienfuegos, playing for the

Boston Red Sox? I'm lost for words. Your father, does he know? Does Cuba know?"

"Nobody knows, Liliana. Just you."

"When will I see you?"

"Soon. Nothing is stopping us now."

"Of course, Pedro. The sooner, the better. Can you come and see me?"

Pedro put Liliana on speaker phone, and looked towards Lily. She spoke.

"Dr. Sánchez, we think it would be good for Pedro to see you. He has time to do that before we begin training, but, please, you must promise to take care of him."

"Of course."

"So, we will book a ticket for him to fly to Newfoundland tomorrow, Dr. Sánchez. Does that work for you?"

Liliana reached for her calendar and stopped cold—nothing was more important than Pedro.

"Tomorrow is perfect, I will pick him up at the airport. Please send me the details: my email address is lsanchez@mun.ca."

"Got it. Tomorrow, then."

In the background, Pedro spoke up.

"Liliana, *te amo.*"

"*Te amo,* Pedro."

It had been more than twenty years since Liliana had thought about baseball. In Cuba, her team, the Guerreros, now defunct, were Havana's second team, leftovers from before the revolution. For Liliana, following the Guerreros was as much about loving the underdog as it was about the game. Even the underdog could gain momentum or, as the Cuban commentators called it, *impulso.* Physicists tried to explain *impulso* by using formulas of mass and speed, but Liliana believed it was more than that. *Impulso* belonged to the unknown, a force beyond the worlds of Einstein or Newton. Liliana loved the mystery, but she also loved the game. It filled her senses, the sights, sounds and smells. And she felt it too. When the Guerreros won, which was seldom, she was euphoric, but when they lost, it hurt. The pain of her team losing didn't make her bleed, but it was real. Physical pain, mental pain and emotional pain all came from the same source deep in the psyche of every living thing. Much about pain was known, much remained to be discovered. But Liliana was more interested in the practical than the theoretical. She wanted to turn the pain off, and she knew how to do that. She knew how to turn off the pain.

Pedro was coming. She would have to divide her time between the person she cared for most and the experiment that defined her life. She wanted to give her undivided attention to both, but that wasn't possible. And then, in a moment of lucidity, it came to her: this wasn't a problem at all, it was an opportunity. Pedro could be part of the trial. If there was one thing her trial lacked, it was endorsement; nothing convinced people like an endorsement, particularly when delivered by the famous.

Liliana smiled to herself. Her problem was really a blessing.

Her life was coming together. She had freedom of mind, she loved the place they called Newfoundland and the thought of seeing Pedro made her heart stir. Her life's work was about to play out in front of her. *Impulso.*

The rain was turning to snow.

23

Constable O'Neil had never met Caleb, and he didn't really care about the blind man and his dog. Right now, all he really cared about was saving his own ass. Myrick said he would deal with the Cubans if O'Neil got the job done. Myrick's exact words had been "Just get Caleb Buckle off the street. I don't care how."

O'Neil was on Water Street just east of Prescott when he pulled up to the curb. He could see the harbour and what looked like snow swirling through the Narrows. Pedestrians turned up their collars and doubled their speed. O'Neil got out of the car and walked slowly; he didn't want to alarm anyone. Not far from Solomon's Lane, he turned into a back alley where Caleb Buckle hung out. Myrick was sure he'd be there, and sure enough, there he was, curled up in his sleeping bag with the dog by his side. The two of them sound asleep. Or so it seemed, at least. O'Neil shuffled over to them.

Blackjack stirred and growled.

Caleb came alive too.

"Who's there, what do you want?"

"Constable O'Neil with the RNC, just checking to see that you're okay. That's all."

"I'm fine, now get the hell out of here."

"Actually, there's one more thing."

O'Neil unhooked his handcuffs from his belt.

Caleb heard the clink. "Oh, no you don't. Blackjack!"

Blackjack growled and bared his teeth.

The cop was coming closer. "Don't fuck with me, I'm warning you."

The boots were still moving. One moment more and the cop would be on top of him. Caleb snapped his fingers. Blackjack lunged, sinking his teeth into O'Neil's pants. O'Neil yelled and tried to push Blackjack away, but Blackjack had him solid.

"Jesus fuck, Caleb, call him off!"

Caleb knew most of the cops around here. He didn't know any O'Neil. He hesitated. Maybe somebody had come to rob him.

O'Neil drew his baton and hit the dog on the back of his neck.

Blackjack released his grip, howled and dropped to the ground.

"What the fuck have you done? Blackjack, Blackjack!"

Blackjack didn't move.

Caleb rushed towards O'Neil and started swinging wildly.

"You bastard, you fucking bastard. Blackjack—Blackjack, where are you?"

Just as Caleb was bending down to find his dog, O'Neil grabbed Caleb's arms and cuffed him. "Fuck you, O'Neil, fuck you."

"Let's check your pockets, Caleb. See what goodies you got."

"You got no reason to search me, I ain't done nothin' wrong."

"What's this—oxy? You got a doctor? Ha. I fuckin' doubt it. Who's givin' you this shit, Caleb?"

Caleb decided to remain silent.

"Maybe Blackjack knows."

"Leave the dog alone. The pills were a gift."

"Yeah, sure, Caleb, a fucking gift. Everybody's out there giving away their oxy."

"It's true, a gift—from a friend."

"Bullshit, Caleb. I'm taking you in—possession and resisting arrest. As for this piece of shit, assaulting a police officer. They'll be looking for a box for him."

For the first time in his life, Caleb felt alone and afraid. He started kicking wildly, screaming, "Myrick, you bastard!"

24

Pedro removed the map from the seat pocket in front of him and spread it on his lap. He could hardly believe the size of Newfoundland and Labrador; it was more than four times the size of his homeland. He had pictured Liliana living on an island smaller than Cuba, and much colder. Snow, igloos and possibly giant white bears.

Pedro loved the window seat. At four thousand feet, the landscape was like a green carpet that was slowly turning white. Snow. He couldn't wait to throw a snowball.

The plane made its final swing and St. John's came into view, stretching back from its nestled harbour over hills until it reached a whitening forest. Outside the harbour was a restless black sea. Pedro had never seen black water; in Cuba, the ocean was blue, sometimes green. He sat back in the seat and closed his eyes. What a strange place: black and white.

As the landing gear locked into place, he looked out again through the little window. Great splashes of colour spread across the hills in the form of brightly painted houses. In Havana, colour had all but disappeared. Even its colourful leader was grey, just like the ideology that had promised so much. It had been a good fight but an unfair one: the neighbourhood bully had blockaded the little island and left it to die.

Pedro's throwing arm had given him hope and a sense of self-worth. When he was a child, he was always the first player chosen for a pick-up game of *béisbol.* It wasn't long before the word spread about the arm of Pedro Cienfuegos.

Later, lifting heavy cases of rum onto a truck made him strong. It wasn't a great job, but it was a job and the occasional bottle of Havana Club made it back to his flat.

The airplane touched down and taxied towards the terminal. Pedro wondered if he would recognize Liliana. It had been twenty-eight years since they had seen each other. He made his way up the jet bridge and followed the crowd to the arrival area.

He quickly scanned the group of people waiting for friends and relatives. One woman stood back from all the rest. Her shoulder-length hair hadn't changed, neither had the soft smile and perfect posture. The long dress threw him; he didn't recall ever seeing her in a dress. But it was Liliana. It had to be.

Their silent embrace seemed to last forever.

Liliana spoke first. "Pedro, I am so happy to see you. Welcome to Newfoundland."

"*Gracias. Ha pasado mucho tiempo.*" Getting the words past the lump in his throat was hard.

"Yes, way too long. You look good, Pedro."

"*Gracias. Igualmente.* Married?"

"No, too busy. What about you?"

"No, I am also too busy." Pedro grabbed his bag from the conveyor belt. "You have rum here?"

"*Sí*, Pedro. You will like this place."

"*Cervaza?*"

"Yes, beer. St. John's has everything, Pedro."

"Like Boston?"

"Well, yes. Sort of."

The automatic door opened, and the cold air hit his face.

"Snow!"

Liliana giggled as Pedro dropped his suitcase, scooped up some snow, compressed it in his bare hands, found his target and let fly.

"Bullseye!"

A few travellers applauded the throw. Others just shook their heads. Pedro smiled and reached for his green and yellow beads.

"My beads, my beads are gone!" Cuban's most famous baseball player dropped to his knees and began groping around in the snow. A street lamp suddenly came on and Pedro looked up: Elegguá, was there, in the light diffused by falling snow, holding his staff.

Pedro laughed and clapped his hands. "It's Elegguá, Liliana—he's checking on me."

Liliana saw nothing, but she knew Elegguá was there—because Pedro believed that he was.

Pedro reached down inside his shirt; the necklace was there. It had broken but the beads had not come off.

"Here it is, it's here in my shirt."

Pedro looked back up at the streetlight. Elegguá was still there. Laughing.

Luke hadn't told Angéline that he had dumped his oxy. There wasn't any need; he had made his decision. He believed in Liliana, and hanging onto the pills was hanging onto the past. He had had enough of that.

Angéline slipped into bed. She sighed with the simple pleasure of wrapping her arms around Luke.

"I love you, Luke, and, believe me, I'm with you every step of the way. One hundred percent. I know you've tried before, but I'm sure this will work; for some reason, I believe in Liliana too. I'm sorry for being such a pain in the ass at her office, but I was concerned about you. About us."

"Thank you, Angel. We're fine, and we'll be finer when I'm clean. I put five thousand of the cash in the bank today."

It was morning, but Angéline had no desire to leave the bed. Instead, she lay on her back letting her thoughts take their course. Once she had believed that not having enough money was at the root of her dreams, that and being homesick for New Orleans. And not having any work: that was like living a half-life. But her days were spent making up for the sleep she missed the night before.

She was worried sick about Luke's addiction. She had faith in his resolve, but flecks of doubt kept creeping in. His track record wasn't good: he had tried to quit three times before and had lost to the opiate. Now he was in way over his head, about to give up his pills and replace them with a mystery woman from Cuba. Angéline wasn't the jealous type, but she couldn't help but wonder. Liliana was ten years older than Luke, but she was intelligent and beautiful and had a good job. Maybe they were planning to run off together, and the money was guilt money. Maybe Luke couldn't handle the dreams anymore.

"Oh, there you are."

Luke held up a bag of coffee.

"Ethiopian."

"Nice."

Angéline got up, put on her robe and followed him barefoot to the kitchen. Luke brewed the coffee, made eggs and toast and brought breakfast to the table.

"Our pillows, how did they end up on the floor?"

Angéline covered her smile; her eyes blinked between her spread fingers.

"Guess you put them there—in case I fell off the bed."

"Or perhaps we slid off the bed and took the pillows with us?"

Angéline burst out laughing and Luke raised his eyebrows. It was time to tell her. Luke stood up and posed like a bodybuilder. "No pill this morning and I feel fine."

Angéline's shoulders straightened and her face suddenly became sombre. "A little overconfident, don't you think?"

"No, ready, that's all."

"I think you're ready too, but I want to be there, like I said, every step of the way."

"You will be there, Angel."

"I mean, I want to go to the meetings. I want to see what's going on. I'm worried about this. I'm worried about you."

"I don't think so, Angel. I don't think that can happen. Let's see what Liliana says."

"No, Luke, we won't see what she says. I'm going and that's it."

26

Pedro poured a drink of rum and sat down next to a window that overlooked the harbour and city. The place was bigger than he imagined. And newer. He'd gone from a stainless-steel airport to what looked like a spaceship on a hill. He wondered how Havana had gotten so far behind. Still, though, he wouldn't be moving here. Not to this frozen outpost. No matter how modern it was.

"Hey, Liliana, come sit down."

"I'll be right there. Just fixing your necklace."

"Gracias."

"How is your father, Pedro?"

"He's well. Busy with state affairs, you know. Saw him before I left—he offered me a job."

"What kind of job?"

"Working for the state."

"Obviously you turned him down."

"Yes, and it made him angry. He doesn't understand that I will do what I want, not what I'm told. Besides, I owe him nothing. Not for his work. And not as a father."

Liliana came into the kitchen and put her hand on Pedro's back. "I understand." She took a glass from the cupboard, poured herself a drink of rum and orange juice and went to sit beside her cousin.

Pedro raised his glass. *"Salude.* The only person I owe is you. And that's why I'm here——to pay up. I have money now."

"My dear Pedro, I don't want your money. But there may be a way you can help me."

"Of course."

"Do you have a baseball?"

"Béisbol? Sí."

Pedro went to his bag, took out a baseball and tossed it to Liliana.

"Nice catch."

"Nice throw. Hardly a hundred though."

They grinned at each other. It was as if time had stood still for the last twenty-five years. Connections like theirs were immune to time and space.

Liliana looked over the ball carefully.

"Have you ever removed the outside layer?"

"The outside?"

"Yes, the outside layer. Have you ever peeled it away?"

"No. Why would you want to remove the outside?"

"Let's just say it's part of my trial."

"Drug trial?"

"You might call it that. Oh, one more thing. I need your name."

"Pedro?"

"No, the Great Ciento."

"You are asking for a lot, Liliana. My father wanted my name; I said no. But my name is yours."

"Thank you, Pedro."

"But how will you use a baseball and my name in a drug trial?"

"It's a long story; perhaps we should have another drink."

Pedro nodded. He got up and refilled their glasses.

27

Myrick was scrolling through the RNC's Facebook site looking for the new recruitment video when the news hit.

Fidel Castro, dead at ninety.

Myrick could barely keep his head above the deluge of words used to describe the Cuban leader: hero, dictator, executioner, president, revolutionary, socialist, rebel, communist, victorious, loved, arrogant, tactician, tyrant, soldier, comrade, philosopher, devil, god, brave, charismatic, guerilla, prisoner, opportunist.

The only word that everyone agreed on was *dead*. Almost everyone. For some, Fidel was immortal. After all, he had escaped more than six hundred and thirty assassination attempts.

A heavy knock sounded on Myrick's door.

"Come in."

O'Neil entered the office, a grim look on his face and one pant leg flapping.

"What the hell happened to you?"

"Buckle's dog—tore my pants and grazed my leg."

"You got Caleb?"

"Yeah, locked up."

"The dog?"

"Animal Control has him."

"Anything else?"

O'Neil reached into his tunic pocket, pulled out a bag of pink pills and laid them on Myrick's desk.

"Prescription, but not his. Said someone gave them to him."

"Anyone see the bust?"

"No. Quiet."

"Anything else? And for Christ's sake, O'Neil, don't leave anything out."

"Well, I'm saving the best for last, sir. I told him I was going to give the dog a good hard kick and then use the pepper spray on him, and Buckle spilled the beans. He gave me a name. Probably made up, but I'll check it out."

"A name?"

"Yeah, Delaney. But then Buckle went nuts."

"Delaney? No, doesn't register. Check it out, O'Neil, find this guy."

"Yes, sir."

Myrick took a letter out of his desk, the one with the Beatles on the stamp—how weird was that, the Beatles on a commie stamp?—and slipped it into the shredder.

"Good work, O'Neil." Myrick pressed the button on the shredder. When O'Neil heard the sound of his big fat Cuban mistake dying a quick death, he let himself quietly out of the office.

Myrick's phone rang. He picked it up.

"Hello."

"Yeah, Myrick. William Saunders. How goes the cleanup?"

"Good. Very good!"

"Keep it up. You ever been to Cuba?"

Myrick almost dropped the phone. *Fuck, how could he know about the letter?*

"No, sir. Why do you ask?"

"Just wondering, that's all. You heard about Castro?"

"Yeah, I heard that."

"Well, keep me in the loop."

"Yes, sir."

Myrick felt like a bullet had just grazed him.

28

It was late November, but there were still a few sparrows at the feeder. Liliana liked to watch them darting around while she did the dishes and listened to CBC on her radio.

"Pedro, come quickly!"

Pedro ran to the kitchen.

"After years of false rumours about his death, Fidel Castro, the ailing former leader of Cuba, has died at the age of ninety. Cuban President Raúl Castro announced the death of his brother on Cuban state media. He ended the announcement by shouting the revolutionary slogan: 'Toward victory, always!'

"The death of Castro has prompted celebrations among Cuban exiles in Miami. 'This is the happiest day of my life; Cubans are finally free,' said Orlidia Montells, an 84-year-old woman.

"'The whole world will remember this man,' said reveller Duncy Fajardo near the iconic National Hotel that hosted Ernest Hemingway and Frank Sinatra—and even known mobsters—before Castro's

1959 revolution led to its nationalization. 'He achieved things that nobody else did.'"

Pedro gazed into Liliana's eyes. They seemed blank and wildly alive at the same time.

"Maybe you should call your father, Pedro."

"No, not now."

They looked at each other and raised their mugs.

"To Cuba."

"*Sí*, to Cuba."

"And to you, Liliana. You seem happy in this New-found-land."

The word—words—hit her: *new found land*. It was her home, but it was also what she was in search of. And like John Cabot, five hundred years before, the search was a visionary one. This time the quest was for a place not on the other side of the world, but on the other side of consciousness. Like the island she lived on, it had always been there: you just had to find it.

29

Luke felt like a sleepwalker as he moved towards the Volvo. He had tossed and turned all night, uneasy about the morning meeting with Liliana. Angéline's dream-talking had only made matters worse. He kicked some snow from the car's wheel well. That's all he needed, something else to slow Newton down. She hadn't been working well lately, and the tailpipe was coughing out a bluish haze. He thought about taking her in to the garage, but he dreaded the phone call that ended with the word *thousand.*

Angéline climbed in the passenger side and closed the door. It didn't latch.

"Jesus, Luke, it's frozen."

"We don't have time to mess with it. Just hold it."

"Hold it?"

Angéline slammed the door three times in succession.

"It's frozen. That won't work."

"Tell you what, Luke, I'll drive, you hold the door."

"Sure."

They changed places. Luke pulled firmly on the frozen door, Angéline turned the key. She edged to the end of the frozen driveway. A car was coming up the road; Angéline was sure she could beat it. She stepped hard on the accelerator, Newton inhaled and lunged ahead.

The centrifugal force was too much. Luke lost his grip and the door flew open. Angéline hit the brakes, and the Volvo came to a sudden stop. The door slammed on Luke's shoulder.

"Jesus, Angel, are you trying to kill me?"

"Sorry, Luke. You okay?"

"Think so."

"You sure?"

Luke put both hands on his lower back and groaned.

"Oh Jesus, Luke."

"I'm okay, just get me to Liliana Sánchez."

"Okay, sweetheart. Sorry."

Luke pulled gently on the door. This time it locked securely. Angéline hung her head for a moment, then shrugged her shoulders, grinned at him and put her foot on the accelerator.

Liliana was standing at the door to the building when they arrived. Her half-frame glasses and white lab coat made Luke feel better about the whole thing. She looked so poised, so professional.

"Come in, Luke. I am so happy to see you. And Angéline. It's good that you are here to support Luke." Liliana indicated a corridor to the left of the door. "This way, please."

Halfway down the corridor there was an elevator, which they entered. When the door closed, Liliana leaned over and whispered, "Luke, I have you signed in as a journalist and Angéline as your intern. You're writing an article on our new facility."

They exited the elevator and walked to the end of a hallway. "So, this is our off-campus lab." Liliana scanned her card, and the door opened.

Stainless steel panels and plate-glass cabinets surrounded the room. The furniture had the same clinical look. Comfort was a foreign concept, lost to the bleakness of geometry. What wasn't stainless steel or glass was white, even the fabric on the only comfortable chairs in the room.

"So, this is the brave new world?"

"Well, it's where I work. What do you think, Angéline?"

"Nice." Angéline wanted to question Liliana about more important things than the look of the place, but she decided to remain silent and let things take their course. Besides, her jealousy radar hadn't even blipped.

"Let's have a seat."

They pulled up three chairs around a glass table. Luke's back was to the wall; he had a full view of the lab. Angéline sat on Luke's right and Liliana sat across from them.

"Let me begin by saying that I am honoured that you have decided to participate. And let me reassure you that everything will be fine. Furthermore, if all goes according to plan, you will be free from your addiction as well as the pain that caused it."

Luke nodded. Liliana turned towards Angéline.

"Angéline, I am delighted you came along. In fact, if you hadn't come, I would not have gone ahead with this. Because, for this to work, controlling every variable is important. The only thing I was unsure of was your relationship with Luke. I sensed it was fine, but your being here proves that my intuition was correct. More than anything, you love him, and you want him to be well."

"Of course."

Liliana turned back to Luke.

"Many opiate users only have themselves, and many are without money or homes. And while you may not see it this way, you are one of the lucky ones: you are not alone, you have your own strength and you have Angéline's, you have the desire to quit and you have me. As they say, the stars are aligned."

Angéline liked the way things were going, and she was starting to like Liliana. But there was still one thing left unexplained. And although she had promised herself she would keep mum, suddenly, the words spilled out.

"The formula, how did you get it to Newfoundland?"

Liliana had hoped Luke or Angéline would bring that up.

"Oh yes, the formula."

30

The pews were full in Courtroom Five, mostly with young men with cold eyes and a veneer of don't fuck with me. Next to them sat their bleached-haired girlfriends, who consoled their lovers as if they were royalty. Then there were the scared-shitless first-timers, wardrobes fresh with package wrinkles, accompanied by bewildered parents.

"Order; all rise. Judge Jonathan Sullivan presiding."

Without looking up, Judge Sullivan made his way to the bench and sat down. He shuffled through a few folders and signalled to the court clerk.

Every Monday, Courtroom Five was like a circus; it was arraignment day. Sitting in front of lawyer Mary Clarke, duty counsel, were twenty-two files, each one with a story as long your arm.

Judge Sullivan opened the first folder on his bench.

"Caleb Buckle, first case."

Mary Clarke stood and addressed the court.

"Your Honour, re the matter of Caleb Buckle, one count of possession of a controlled substance for the purpose of trafficking and one count of resisting arrest. Mr. Buckle has requested that I speak on his behalf."

"Go ahead, Ms. Clarke. Is Mr. Buckle present?"

"Yes, Your Honour."

Caleb heard his name and stood up.

"Excuse me, Ms. Clarke, is Mr. Buckle blind?"

"Yes, he is."

"Well then, I'm a little confused. One count of resisting arrest?"

"Well, Your Honour, it seems there was a dog involved."

"So, Ms. Clarke, is the resisting arrest charge against the dog or Mr. Buckle?"

"Your Honour, from what I understand the dog attacked the arresting constable at Mr. Buckle's command."

"Well, that's an interesting point, isn't it? Accomplice to a crime is different, of course, from committing the crime. But, of course, a dog can't be tried for accessory or anything else."

Ms. Clarke smiled. "Of course not, Your Honour, Mr. Buckle wishes to plead guilty to both charges, and, if the Crown is willing, Mr. Buckle would like to set a date for sentencing.

"One other thing, Your Honour, Mr. Buckle has no fixed address, so, if it pleases the court, Mr. Buckle would like to remain in the court's custody until sentencing."

"Request is granted."

Caleb didn't want to speak, but he realized it might be his only chance.

"Your Honour, may I say a few words?"

"Of course, Mr. Buckle."

"Your Honour, my dog is all I have, and now I'm not even sure if he's alive. Your Honour, I can't survive without him, he is my eyes and the only thing that makes sense to me. Can someone let me know where he is and how he is doing?"

"That seems like a fair request. Ms. Clarke, would you please check into that for Mr. Buckle?"

31

Liliana knew that if there was anything that could lead to belief, it was a good story. Entire cultures and religions had been built on stories. Stories so bold that people would kneel and pray to omnipotent unknowns.

"You want to know how I got the formula?"

Liliana walked over to her desk, opened the top drawer, and pulled out a baseball.

"The formula came in this. It was sent to my office by my nephew, Pedro Cienfuegos."

Liliana peeled away the leather cover, which was already unstitched. Beneath the cover were three layers of wrapped thread which Liliana had already cut away, exposing a rubber casing that surrounded a cork ball.

Liliana took the cork ball between her fingers.

"In baseball language, this is called the pill. Using an inert paste, Pedro formed the compound into the shape of the pill.

"He found the compound in a container in our house in Havana. There was a note attached, with me as the contact. So, Pedro concealed the compound in this baseball and mailed it to St. John's.

"Once I received it, all I had to do was analyze the compound and record the chemical structure. I've since made up my own batch of the compound, which I tested on mice and rats. The efficacy rate was higher than Dr. Kolosov and I ever imagined it would be: ninety-five percent effective. With no side effects.

"And now I'm ready to take it to the next level.

"But before I give you the pills, I'd like you to meet my nephew, Pedro. Pedro Cienfuegos is here to tell his story of shoulder pain and alcohol addiction and how he became healed from both afflictions.

"In Cuba, they call him the Great Ciento. He is a pitcher with a fastball of one hundred miles an hour. He may be forty but has found a new game, playing for the Boston Red Sox."

"The Sox?" Luke's face registered shock and disbelief.

"Yes, the contract is signed but not announced yet. But I think you should hear Pedro speak for himself. Let me get him."

The scene had been set, the story told and the medicine ready. Pedro would help confirm everything. It was like Mozart believing in Mesmer.

Liliana opened a door that led to an adjacent room. "Come into the lab, Pedro, and meet Luke and Angéline."

Luke's father, Michael, had followed the Sox because he figured that Boston had to be the most Irish place in North America next to Newfoundland. One of the biggest deals of Michaels's life was going to Boston to see a game at Fenway Park. Fenway Park was the oldest ballpark in the major leagues, greener than a forest in the middle of one of America's oldest cities. It had amassed much baseball lore: the lone red seat, the triangle, Pesky's Pole, Duffy's Cliff, the green monster. And, of course, the curse of the Bambino: the failure of the Sox to win the World Series between 1918 and 2004, supposedly caused by the team's sale of Babe Ruth to the Yankees in 1919. Michael disliked the well-heeled Yankees, except for Yogi Berra, Yankee catcher and manager more famous for his Yogi-isms than his career. Berra once said, 'Baseball is ninety percent mental, and the other fifty percent is physical." It made as much sense as anything. Michael didn't believe in curses; he thought that a curse was merely recurrent doubt, and the only cure for doubt was faith. Someone must have heard Michael's thoughts, for during the 2004 baseball season a gigantic billboard with the words "Keep the Faith" overlooked Fenway Park. The critical ingredient was added, the insidious nature of doubt quenched, and, after eighty-six years, the Boston Red Sox finally won the World Series. Michael Delaney and thousands of others called it the best year of their lives.

Luke was eight when he started following baseball. Sometimes, late at night, if the signal was good, he could pick up a Boston radio station and fall asleep listening to Joe Castiglione calling a game. During post-season games, Luke and his father would raise the Red Sox flag. They were more than fans, they idolized their team. And it brought them together as father and son.

Luke never got to Fenway Park, but he and his friend Mikey Ryan used to stand at the edge of the Narrows in St. John's harbour believing they were Ted Williams and Carl Yastrzemski. With their bats, they hit rocks, one after the other, over the green monster, the left field wall of an imaginary Fenway Park.

Pedro Cienfuegos entered the room. He was a tall man, six-three, fit, dark-skinned. His hair was black and shoulder-length: he looked more like a rock star than a baseball star. He extended his hand to Luke.

"Nice to meet you, Luke.

"Nice to meet you. This is my partner, Angéline LeBlanc."

"Pleasure."

Angéline tilted her head to meet Pedro's eyes. She liked what she saw. "Nice to meet you, Pedro. You have come a long way." His looks were stunning, but there was something about him that was even stronger than his sexual charisma. Whatever it was, Angéline felt drawn to it.

"*Sí*, pitching for the Sox."

"No, I mean to Newfoundland."

"*Sí*, but it has been a much longer journey to the major leagues."

"Your baseball life in Cuba, what was it like?"

"My first memories are playing with Liliana, a cardboard baseball glove and a ball made from rolled fishing net. From there to the streets of Centro Habana, then to the fields. Next thing you know, I'm throwing eighty, ninety, one hundred miles an hour. The Cuban leagues scouted me, and, for the last twenty-five years, I've been pitching for the top Havana team. I throw hard, but only a few pitches. That's usually all I ever need. I'm a closer, a pitcher who's called on in the last inning to finish a game. But, in 2008, chronic pain in my throwing arm finished my career."

"But you're still pitching?"

"*Sí*, I got a job at a rum factory. Liquor was easy to get, so I started drinking heavily and would steal bottles and hide them in the walls of my flat. That's where I found Dr. Kolosov's container. I contacted Liliana and sent the compound to her—concealed in an autographed baseball. Liliana carried out studies and returned some of the compound to me. She wrote instructions on the inside cover of the ball. Within two weeks I gave up drinking and was back on the mound, pitching faster than I ever did before. I also perfected another pitch—the split-finger fastball, which allowed me to mix things up a bit. The Red Sox's scouts heard about me. The Red Sox made me an offer. I accepted."

"Wow, that is quite the journey!"

"Nothing compared to kids on an open raft in the Florida Straits. Perspective, I guess."

"Yeah, I've seen pictures."

Liliana opened her briefcase and pulled out a bottle of pills. She handed them to Luke. "You need to take one a day, preferably in the morning, with food. Have you stopped taking the oxy?"

"Yes."

"That's good. When?"

"Last night."

"How are you doing?"

"Early yet, but a little jittery."

"Take one of these, it will block all the symptoms that you've experienced: the jitteriness, the irritability, the insomnia and the pain."

"Hope so. Here goes."

Luke unscrewed the top of the bottle and reached in for a single pill.

"Jesus, this looks just like my OxyNEOS. Eighty stamped on one side, ON on the other. The same colour." Liliana got him a glass of water and he took the pill.

Angéline examined one of the pills. "Yeah, they look the same."

"A protective measure, that's all. See, Luke has a prescription for OxyNEO 80s: if he's stopped while in possession of something different, it might get difficult."

"You've thought ahead; I like that."

"I have to."

Angeline held out her hand to the famous Cuban baseball player. "Pedro, thank you for being here. If I don't see you again, good luck with the Sox. I'll be watching for you."

"I don't believe in luck. Things happen because of cause and effect. Not luck. Time is the only thing out of a person's control. But with the strength of belief, you can even control time. Do you know Santeria?"

"Santeria, of course. I know it well." Angeline's smile lit up her face and the room. That was the thing about him that had tugged so on her intuition: his spiritual strength.

"Well then, Pedro, please keep Angéline company while I check Luke's vitals."

32

Stories of a hard childhood didn't impress Crown Attorney Garrett Strong. Strong had been a foster child himself and if he could beat the odds, everybody could. That was his theory, anyway. Strong had a yearning for the big time; he just had to do the shit time first. The more scum he could put behind bars, the faster he could climb. He could spout facts and case numbers like they happened yesterday. Many of them had. Cases were piling up on his desk; most of them involved people charged with possession or trafficking of a controlled substance.

His phone rang. "Mr. Strong, Inspector Myrick is here to see you."

"Send him in."

"Come in, Inspector, have a seat. Happy you could make it. So, what's going on at the detachment? Eight new drug files since yesterday. At this rate, I'll need a half dozen more attorneys just to keep up with the mess. Look at my desk. You know me, Myrick, I want to clean it up, but without more prosecutors, we can't do it. I feel like I'm shovelling snow with a broken shovel and another goddamn storm is on the way."

Myrick put it together. Garrett Strong was drowning in files and William Saunders was crying out for more. And he was smack in the middle of it. What was that line, something about not serving two masters because you'd end up hating one of them? But Myrick liked both men.

"Well, Garrett, we're doing our job, that's all."

"Sure, you are, but arresting a homeless blind man? That's a bit much—even by my standards."

"Buckle had a bag of OxyNEOs—prescription stuff."

"Fair enough, but why are you busting every addict on the corner? You know that's not going to clear up the problem, so what in the hell are you people doing?"

Myrick slumped in his chair. "Look, Garrett, I don't know what's going on any more than you do. I don't make policy; that's beyond my pay level."

The Crown attorney rolled his eyes and glanced down at the file on his desk. "Well, can you try to find out who Buckle's supplier is? You think Buckle will bargain with us?"

"Yeah, I think he will. Animal Control has his dog and that dog is all he has in the world. I think we can broker a deal with him."

"Where is Buckle now?"

"He's still in the lockup."

"Make sure they don't put that dog down."

"I will. Hope it's not too late."

33

Every morning, Luke went to the holy cabinet in the kitchen, took out his bottle of sacramental pills and swallowed one. He could feel the chemicals flow through his body like the Holy Ghost.

After two weeks, just as Liliana had promised, he was feeling better than ever before, no withdrawal and no pain. And no side effects. He started to believe in himself again, especially after he gave up alcohol, dope and even tea. He considered giving up coffee, but he figured that Angéline would leave him if he quit that. After all, finding and drinking coffee together was one of their sacred rituals.

"Hey, Mossy, how's it going? Don't suppose you want to go for a run?"

"Running in winter, Luke? Last month you could barely walk to the fridge."

"Feeling better, that's all."

"What's up, a magic pill?"

"Yes. Don't laugh. I can't tell you much, but let me just say I'm part of a drug trial."

"You've given up the oxys?"

"Yeah, I'm off them. You can't tell anyone. I'm only telling you because, well—I love you, man."

"Shit. What kind of pills are you on now anyway, Luke?"

Mossy was laughing, and Luke could tell he was touched, but the guy had spent his adolescence on a fishing boat in Trinity Bay. Any talk of love on that boat, among those men, would have ended badly.

"How's Angéline?"

"She's fine, still having those dreams, though. We've got some money now, so we're going to deal with that."

"Make sure you give her my best. Let's all get together sometime—supper, whatever?"

"Sure. But what do you say to a run this afternoon? Not far, just from my house up to Fort Amherst and back."

"Sure, why not."

"Thanks. Listen, Mossy, I know I've been a bit of an asshole lately, but opiate addiction is hard stuff. The only time you feel okay is when the oxy is pumping through your veins. When it wears off you feel miserable again. So, you take another pill. The cycle never ends. But now I'm clean. I haven't taken an oxy in ten days."

"That's great news, Luke, see you in a bit."

Within an hour, Mossy was at Luke's house. Mossy didn't drop by as much as he used to. He was finding it difficult to deal with Luke's anxious and irritable behaviour. But today was different, it was just like old times, the two of them telling stories and laughing to beat the band.

"Remember that trip to the island when . . ."

There was a knock on the door. A loud knock that seemed to reverberate inside Luke's head. "Jesus Christ, Mossy, if that's the Jehovah's Witnesses again this week . . ." Although they didn't usually use that much force on Luke's red door; they knocked as politely as they dressed and spoke. He expelled a long, irritated sigh and opened the door. Two police officers stood there, a man and a woman.

"Are you Mr. Luke Delaney?"

"I am."

"Mr. Delaney, I'm Constable O'Neil and this is Constable Cooper. We have a warrant to search these premises. Part II of the Controlled Drugs and Substances Act."

"What the hell?"

"Here's the warrant."

"What's your name, sir?" Mossy decided it wasn't his good-looking, intelligent face that had prompted this inquiry from Constable Cooper. She wasn't smiling, for one thing.

"Mossy."

"Mossy what?"

"Unless I'm under arrest, it's none of your business."

"I'm authorized to search anyone found in a drug house, Mossy. Stand still."

She patted him down like an expert, because she was one. Mossy felt used. And confused. "Luke, what the hell is going on?"

"Don't know."

O'Neil made his way into the kitchen and started opening cabinets. Within a few minutes, he returned to the living room. "Hey, Cooper, a bottle of OxyNEOs. The same as Buckle had on him."

He turned to Luke. "These yours, Mr. Delaney?"

"Yes, sir."

"Prescription?"

"Yes, sir."

"You taking these?"

Luke started to say yes, but he'd just told Mossy he'd given up the pills. And if he said no, the officers would be all over him. He thought about telling the truth, but that wasn't an option. No way would he expose Liliana.

There was a sound of drawers opening and closing in Luke and Angéline's bedroom. Luke winced; he knew what was coming down the tubes. Constable Cooper's boots clattered over the stairs. She was holding up an envelope as she entered the kitchen.

"What have you got there, Cooper?"

"Seems like Mr. Delaney likes to keep a lot of cash around."

The two police officers looked at Luke. Cold-eyed stares. Luke suddenly felt a small, sharp pain in his lower back. Jesus Christ.

"Mr. Delaney, I am arresting you under section 5(2) of the Controlled Drugs and Substances Act for possession of oxycodone for the purpose of trafficking.

"Do you want to contact your lawyer, Mr. Delaney? I can give you the number for legal aid if you need it. They have lawyers available twenty-four seven."

Constable O'Neil took a piece of cardboard out of his tunic pocket and began reading it out loud. "'I wish to give you the following warning: You need not say anything. You have nothing to hope from any promise or favour and nothing to fear from any threat whether you say anything. Anything you do or say, may be used as evidence.'"

He looked at Luke. "Do you understand?"

"Yes."

Constable Cooper took out a pair of handcuffs and snapped them on Luke's wrists. Then she turned to Mossy.

"Sir, we don't need you right now, but don't be surprised if you hear from us again. Constable O'Neil will take your contact information."

Luke turned his head. Mossy was standing a few feet from him, looking as if he had turned to clay.

"Mossy, let Angéline know what happened. Tell her I'll be fine. I'll call a lawyer."

"Jesus, Luke, what in the hell is going on?"

"All you need to know is I'm innocent. I can explain everything."

"Then call Alex Caddigan—he's a friend of mine and the best lawyer in town."

34

Pedro Cienfuegos and Angéline LeBlanc's conversation at the lab had continued over the ensuing weeks at various coffee shops around the city. They talked about hurricanes and sugarcane and the warm breezes of the south. She told him about New Orleans, the music and the food and the feel of it; he told her about Cuba, how things were in that country that was so close to her own but so shrouded in the secrecy of communism that it seemed far off and dream-like. They spoke of the American and Cuban détente. And how they both loved flamenco. Pedro loved watching women dance flamenco in a bar after a baseball game; often, he did not leave alone, but with some fiery *mujer bella* in a fiery dress. Angéline had dreamt of being a flamenco dancer as a child; she had taken lessons as a young woman. She still had her red-and-black flamenco dress and the long silver and garnet earrings that her mother had left her. She loved the way they spun as she swayed and stamped in time to the music. Sometimes she put everything on and pinned up her hair and danced for Luke in the living room, the stereo on full blast. Luke liked the way her hands moved like a sea swell, and, in an instant, from enchantment to fury. Like a rogue wave in the night. At least, that's how he put it. Perhaps now that his back was better, she could teach him some steps.

"I am sure I will miss my homeland when I settle in America. And Boston is cold, yes?"

"In the winter, yes."

"Have you ever been to Cuba?"

"I've wanted to go, but the travel ban prevented it. I could go from Canada, but we can't afford it right now. My mother's great-grandparents worked there in the 1920s, cutting sugarcane."

"In Cuba?"

"Yes. Their names were Emmanuel and Amma Dumois, and they moved from Haiti to Santiago de Cuba to cut cane. When the market for sugarcane crashed in the 1930s, they were kicked out of the country, partly because they were black—well, mulatto, anyway—and partly because the sugar industry was in a slump. Most of the Haitians went back to Haiti, but for some reason my ancestors went to New Orleans."

"Maybe someday you will finally get to my country."

"It's strange, two people from the south meeting on an island in the North Atlantic."

"Not really. We never know where life will take us, or who we'll meet. With any luck, people who will give us new ideas and perspectives. That is more likely to happen if there is freedom, something that the Cuban people have not known for many years. But things are changing, and I live in the hope that my people will be free again. If they are lucky, they too will meet beautiful people like you and Luke."

"Thank you, Pedro. That's very kind. Will you ever go back to Cuba?"

"*Sí*. I need the nourishment that only my home can offer. And I need my religion. But wherever I am, Orula and Elegguá are always with me, and I will always honour my beliefs and practice them. If I don't, my good fortune will end."

"But, Pedro, that is how I feel, exactly. Only I am not practising them, not living my beliefs like you are."

Angéline and Pedro leaned closer over the table that separated them and began talking about their beliefs. Beliefs that had sailed the Atlantic in slave ships and landed in the new world, and had changed in response to Western culture and its religions. Pedro's Santería was a secretive practice and Angéline's New Orleans voodoo an open spiritualism. But they were the same in their essence: they connected the believer with the unseen forces and helped her or him to transcend the mundane.

"Pedro, it's so good to talk with someone who shares similar beliefs. I love Luke to pieces, but I miss my home and my spiritual practice. Luke is secular, although sometimes he and I go to Mass. Mostly only at Christmas and Easter, so it's basically just childhood nostalgia for both of us. I need more than that."

"Then, *cariña*, you must start." Pedro took off his green and yellow orisha beads, placed them in Angéline's hands, and placed his hands over hers.

"Oh, Pedro, I can't. Not your beads . . ."

"I can get a new set in America, Angéline. With the money I am now making, I can get beads with diamonds in them, if I want them. But that would not please Orula any more than these do. Less, perhaps. I like you, Angéline, and I know how you have been suffering from your dreams. I believe these can help you. Set you back on the path. Please, take them. For Luke's sake as well."

Angéline 's eyes welled up and the tears ran down her cheeks. Pedro wiped them, away, smiling. He leaned back and looked at her.

"No more dreams, Angéline. Wear my beads, pray, make a little shrine in your home. Let the gods back into your heart."

35

Alex Caddigan's nickname was 'Streetcar."
Some people said that was because he was built like
one, others said it was because he'd been around when
the trolleys rolled through the old city. Bolstering the
streetcar moniker was the seventy-eight-year-old
lawyer's excruciatingly slow pace. A mammoth white
beard made up for the lack of hair on his head. His
eyebrows were also thick and white. The roots of a
tree in an Irish meadow would have been a fitting
dwelling place for him, but it would have had to be a
Douglas fir: at five feet eleven inches, Alex Caddigan
was two hundred and fifty pounds.

Once he'd explained his lateness to a judge by
saying he'd been in another court. "The food court,
Mr. Caddigan?" asked the judge.

Caddigan's weight suited him; it fitted his
folksy, easygoing demeanour. He charmed everyone,
even the repeat offenders, whom he knew by their first
names, just like he knew the judges by theirs. The
other lawyers said Caddigan was like a pool shark.
He'd bait you with his apparent good-naturedness and

seeming incompetence and then take you down with a series of well-aimed shots.

Luke was in the interview room when a uniformed police officer opened the door.

"Mr. Delaney, your lawyer is here. Would you like to see him?"

"Please."

Alex Caddigan stepped into the room with his hand outstretched and Luke got up and shook it. Caddigan was as big in person as he was on TV.

"So, Mr. Delaney—may I call you Luke?"

"Yes."

"You called about a charge laid against you— possession of a controlled substance for the purpose of trafficking. Is that correct?"

"Yes."

"And you'd like to hire me as counsel for your defence?"

"Yes, but what's it going to cost me?"

"My rates are comparable to every other firm's. And I've had far more experience than most lawyers, because I'm old enough to be a grandfather to most of them. I focus entirely on drug-related matters. I know this stuff inside out.”

“How much?”

“Two hundred and fifty an hour.”

“Sweet Jesus! I can’t afford that.”

“I usually charge three hundred, but you’re a friend of Mossy’s so I’m giving you a deal. Trafficking is serious stuff, Luke. I haven’t received disclosure, but from what I understand you were apprehended with a pill bottle containing twenty-eight OxyNEOs? Is that correct?”

“Yes.”

“Were the pills prescribed to you?”

“It’s a little more complicated than that.”

“Complicated or not, I’ll need to know everything.

“A criminal conviction for trafficking a Schedule 1 narcotic is serious business. And in case you don’t know, there’s a saying in the legal profession, ‘What do you call a possession charge without a Charter challenge? Guilty.’ What I’m saying is, you’ll need one hell of a good explanation to get away with this. Of course, there is always a chance that we can bargain for the lesser charge."

"Jesus, I thought you were on my side. I'll be pleading not guilty."

"Okay, tomorrow morning, 9:30, Courtroom Seven. We'll enter your plea. The duty officer said you were free to go. Want a lift home?"

"Sure, thanks."

36

Angéline couldn't believe the change in Luke. He was like the Luke of old. They were both starting to enjoy life again. She looked at the light sprinkling of snow on the South Side Hills and thought how beautiful it was. And she hated snow. The profound change in Luke made her a freer person, free to see the beauty in most things. And her spirit was loosening up for other reasons. Keeping one hand tight on the wheel of the car, she reached inside the neck of her sweater with the other and stroked the yellow and green necklace.

Liliana was already seated when Angéline walked into the restaurant. She couldn't wait to tell her about Luke's amazing recovery, and her own.

Liliana rose up out of her chair when she saw Angéline approaching the table. "Angéline! How are you, how is Luke?"

"Luke is absolutely marvellous, Liliana. Better than I've ever seen him. You have worked a miracle.

"As for me, I'm freaking marvellous too, thanks to your cousin. We talked about our beliefs, our spiritual roots, and he gave me his orisha necklace. And I have not had one single bad dream since! He told me. . ." The sound of Robert Johnson's "Crossroad Blues" began issuing out of Angéline's purse. She zipped it open, took out her phone, made a face at Liliana. "Could be Luke—I'll just check." She glanced at the number. "That's odd—why would Mossy be calling me? Sorry, Liliana, but I should take this. I have a bad feeling."

"You should always go with your instincts, *cariña*."

"Where's Luke? I thought he was with you?"

"Luke's okay, he's fine."

"Where is he?"

"I'm not sure how to say this—Luke's been arrested."

A blank look filled Angéline's face, and behind it was the whiteness of shock. It took all she had to push the words from her mouth.

"Arrested? For what?"

"Best as I can tell, trafficking drugs."

"That can't be, there must be some mistake. Where is he?"

"He was at the detachment, but he should be back home by now."

"Thanks, Mossy—got to go." Angéline hung up and called their home number.

"Hello."

"Luke—you okay?"

"I'm fine. I guess Mossy told you."

"Yes, he called a few minutes ago."

"And Liliana, is she with you?"

"Yes."

"I'm innocent, Angel. I can't believe this is happening."

"Don't worry, I'm coming home right now."

"May I speak with Liliana?"

"Sure."

"Luke, Angéline had you on speaker phone. I'm so sorry to hear this."

"No worries, I'm innocent. But they have your pills."

"*They?*"

"The police."

"Oh no."

37

Alex Caddigan, Luke and Angéline agreed to meet the following morning at the Atlantic Place food court, several floors below the court where Luke would be facing a judge.

Caddigan was already half-way through a large smoothie, chasing it with a black coffee, when Luke and Angéline arrived.

"I hope you're right, Luke, about him being the best. Because he looks like a homeless guy."

"Give him a chance, Angel."

"A chance? This isn't a bingo game, Luke, it's your life. I hope Mossy's got his head on straight when it comes to Caddigan, because he looks like a long shot to me."

"Shh!"

"Have a seat, Luke, Angéline. Can I get you a coffee?"

Angéline wanted to wipe off the red juice dripping down Caddigan's beard, but she restrained herself. If he didn't clean himself up before they went into court, however, she'd march him into the men's room herself.

"No thanks. It's almost 9:30. We'd better get going."

"So it is. And security's tighter than a frog's arse."

Angéline rolled her eyes. Two hundred and fifty an hour for this?

They took the elevator upstairs. Outside the courtroom, Angéline and Luke emptied their pockets, removed their boots and passed through the X-ray machine. Caddigan flashed his card and circumvented the security protocol. The three of them entered Courtroom Seven and sat down.

Luke looked around the corral of miscreants. A couple of them were sporting bruises and bandages from the night before. One guy was fast asleep.

"All rise. Judge Sheila Mahoney presiding."

Judge Mahoney's black robe was in stark contrast to her scarlet sash and the white tie that hung boldly around her neck. Her closely cropped white hair and red-framed glasses made her look almost fashionable. Luke hoped she was also intelligent and compassionate.

Judge Mahoney didn't even glance at the courtroom's occupants. She went straight to the bench and summoned the court clerk for the first name on the docket.

"Lucas Delaney, Your Honour."

Alex Caddigan stepped forward from a cluster of lawyers to the front of the courtroom and addressed the judge.

"Your Honour, I'll be representing Mr. Delaney."

"Is Mr. Delaney in the courtroom?"

Alex Caddigan turned towards Luke who was sitting three pews behind and beckoned to him. Angéline took Luke's hand and squeezed it. Luke walked up to the dock and stood facing the judge.

"Mr. Delaney, you've been charged under Part I, Subsection 5 (1) of the Controlled Drugs and Substances Act: one count of possession for the purpose of trafficking. How do you plead?"

"Your Honour, this is some kind of mistake."

"Mr. Delaney, you will have lots of time to argue your side when the case goes to trial. This is only a reading of the charges."

Alex Caddigan turned his head and raised his eyebrows at Luke.

"Not guilty, Your Honour."

"Your Honour, if it pleases the Court and the Crown, I'd like to expedite this case. I will be leaving the country in a month, and not returning for a year."

"I see no problem with that, Mr. Caddigan. And the Crown?"

"Fine, Your Honour."

"Can we agree on a date?"

"December 17, Your Honour." The Crown attorney looked bored, possibly even hung over.

Alex Caddigan looked at Luke, who turned towards Angéline, who nodded.

"December 17, it is. Courtroom Five."

"Your Honour, disclosure will be in counsel's hands as soon as possible.

"Thank you. Next file, please."

"The Court calls Cody Chafe."

There was no response.

"Mr. Chafe does not appear to be present,
Your Honour."

"This is Mr. Chafe's third chance. Please issue
a warrant for his arrest."

Luke and Angéline followed Alex Caddigan to
his office on Duckworth Street.

The steps to the third-floor office were steep,
twisting and narrow. Caddigan often lost his step or
his breath or both before he got to the top.

"Here we are." Caddigan reached for the
doorknob and used it as a support for his breathless,
tired body.

Angéline whispered in Luke's ear. "Haven't
paid him, have you? Looks like he's going to collapse."

Caddigan opened the office door. "Come in,
sit down.

"I'll be getting the disclosure—the Crown's
side of the story—in a couple of days. Right now, I'd
like to hear your side, Luke."

Luke gave the attorney a grim look. "My 'side' of the story happens to be the truth."

"That's good, and I believe you, but we'll need to prove it. You do realize that you were caught with a bottle of pills and a large quantity of cash."

"Yes, but I can explain all that."

"Fair enough. We can meet again in a couple of days; by then I should have the disclosure.

"One question, before you leave. If the pills were prescription, how are you managing without them?"

"I'm doing okay. I can get more pills from . . . the doctor. The pills the cops took, where are they?" Luke hoped Caddigan hadn't noticed his pause before the words *the doctor*. Well, Liliana did have a PhD, so he wasn't lying.

"On their way to Montreal for analysis. The results will accompany the Crown's disclosure. I'll call you when it arrives."

Shit. What would they make of Liliana's concoction? Did this mean he was in serious trouble or that he would get off scot-free? But Liliana wasn't a doctor. Had she given him some kind of super narcotic? What kind of idiot was he, trusting a foreign woman from a shady communist state? He heard himself groan out loud.

Scot-free. The word had nothing to do with the Scots, it was derived from the Scandinavian *skat*, which meant "tax." Tax-free.

"One more question, Alex. Are lawyer's fees taxed?"

"Fifteen percent, just like everything else."

Angéline did a quick calculation: forty-five dollars an hour in taxes. That was twice her hourly wage at the last job she had.

"We'd better get going, Luke. You're a nice man, Alex, but way too expensive to hang out with."

38

Caleb Buckle had a bed, a bathroom and three meals a day at the city lock-up. Being blind, he didn't have to deal with the look of the place, but his sense of smell was keener than most people's. Unfortunately.

"Hey, Caleb, you've got a visitor."

"I don't need no lawyer."

"It's me—Myrick."

"What the fuck do you want?"

"Got something for you."

"I don't need nothing from you. Get out."

Myrick motioned to the guard. "Bring him in."

The guard released the leash and Blackjack raced to Caleb's cell. He flung his whole weight against the bars, barking and whimpering.

"Blackjack!"

Myrick wasn't about to get all warm and fuzzy.

"Guard, you can leave. I want some time with Mr. Buckle."

"Sure."

"So, Caleb, this guy, Delaney—tell me about him."

"Fuck you, Myrick."

"Seems like you don't get it. You know what happens when a dog attacks a police officer? So, Caleb, is Delaney a supplier? You tell me, and I can call somebody."

Myrick opened the cell door. Blackjack ran through and jumped on Caleb like as if life depended on it. It did.

Myrick snapped a couple of photographs with his phone.

"And, Caleb, check the dog's collar. You'll find a special present from me."

When Myrick returned to the station he had all the information he needed. And a photograph of a blind man reaching for his beloved dog. The local paper would swallow it up. There was nothing like a good-news story these days. Even if it wasn't exactly true.

Carol Stapleton would be sending him flowers; even the cop haters would be choking up.

39

Luke wondered how often in an adult life everything lined up: good health, enough money, the right livelihood. And a mate who loves you above everything. Luke was close to having it all, and now the one thing that he had never given much thought to was about to bring it all down. The law was part of another world, something that happened to other people. Not him.

When other people believe you are guilty, you start to question yourself. Paranoia sets in and reality becomes skewed. You start seeing things that aren't there. Luke knew that using his cell phone could be unsafe, so he began using the old phone booths that still stood in a parts of the downtown. Luke knew that the police couldn't wiretap a public phone, but what he didn't know was that video surveillance of the phone booths was twenty-four seven. Someone had to care for the past—at least that was the story.

Luke inserted twenty-five cents and dialled Liliana's number.

"Hello, Liliana."

"Hey Liliana, it's Luke."

"Oh Luke, my god—are you okay?"

"Sort of. Listen, we need to talk—can you meet me today somewhere?"

"I can meet you now, if that's good with you."

"Great. I'm at a phone booth on the corner of Gower and Ordnance. There's a coffee shop right next to it. I'll be at a table by the fireplace."

"Okay, I'll be right there."

Ten minutes later, Liliana came through the door of the coffee shop.

"That was fast; please sit down. I bought you a coffee."

"Thanks, Luke. How are you doing?"

"These charges, I'm worried about them."

"No need to worry."

"What do you mean?"

"All you need to know is that the contents of the pills are legal. They'll drop the charges when they get the analysis."

"Are you sure of that?"

"Absolutely certain."

"So, what's in the pills?"

"If I told you, it might compromise your recovery."

"That's a strange answer."

"I know, but that's just the way it is. You need to trust me."

"I do."

"Luke, listen, even though the contents are legal, the police will want to know where the pills came from. And why they look like Oxy. You need to give them my name."

"I can't do that after all you've done for me."

"Believe me, it's not betrayal. I can deal with it."

40

Alex's mahogany bookcases had fallen well short of their role. A dozen half-opened law books with sticky notes hanging off the pages were scattered around the room. Papers and folders covered the surface of his roll-top desk. A single folder with a cast iron model of a streetcar on it sat alone on the window sill. One wall was covered with a patchwork of Newfoundland art, every piece unique and crying out to be by itself, to be seen as its creator saw it. Luke figured Alex must see something in chaos that was not apparent to most people.

One of Alex's colleagues said that if only Alex could find the sugar, he could spin legal jargon like cotton candy and make it sound just as sweet. In their first meeting, Luke had barely kept up with what Alex was saying; thank god for Google. Luke had used it to unravel the jargon bit by bit and get a sense of what was going on.

Today, the main word was *disclosure,* and the message was clear.

"Jesus, Alex, *trafficking.* This is crazy."

"According to the police, somebody by the name of Caleb Buckle said he received some pills from you. Is that true?"

"Oh, Jesus, no."

"No, he didn't receive pills from you?"

"No—I mean, yes, I gave him some pills. They were a gift. I just like the old guy, that's all. You must know Caleb and his dog; they're permanent fixtures downtown. His back is bad from sleeping rough. And he helped me out one time—nothing illegal."

"Fair enough, but the Crown sees matters a little differently. And there's also the issue of the large supply of cash in your house. Are you able to explain that?"

"Well, that's a little more difficult to explain."

"The only way I can defend you is if I know everything. Let me be clear, I believe in your innocence, but I need to know all of it.

"One more thing, Luke. The drug analysis is back. The pills Caleb Buckle had in his possession were OxyNEOs, the pills at your place were milk sugar."

"Milk sugar?"

"Yes, milk sugar, otherwise known as lactose, but these pills were branded the same as OxyNEOs. The Crown suspects you may be selling fake Oxy. And then there's the cash. Want to tell me about it?"

Luke felt like a rat in a corner. Had Liliana been deceiving him all along? Pedro too? His stomach felt like a horse had given it a good kick. But he'd been healed of his addiction. Luke felt like a small, sick child who just wanted to be home in bed. With his mother doting on him, hot chocolate and soothing words.

"Your story has more holes than Swiss cheese, Luke. If we're going to win this, you have to come clean."

"Okay, Alex. But even for me, there are missing pieces.

"I know this doctor. Actually, she's a pharmacologist. Her name is Liliana Sánchez."

Alex's phone rang.

"Hold that thought, Luke."

Luke listened and watched. After a few minutes, and a few short sentences from his lawyer to the invisible person on the other end of the line, Alex Caddigan's face grew sombre. He hung up the phone and looked at Luke.

"That was Garrett Strong, the Crown attorney. Apparently, Caleb Buckle died last night in his cell. Until they get the autopsy results they won't know the cause of death. But if the death is related to opioid use, the Crown is considering charging you with manslaughter."

"That's crazy. This can't be true." Not a horse, a rhinoceros must have got him in the gut. Luke wanted to put his head on Alex's desk and cry, but if he did that maybe he'd never find his head again in all the mess.

"We had better prepare for the worst, Luke. So, tell me everything. Everything!"

41

Pedro reached across the table and placed his hands over Angéline's. "Angéline, your dreams are yours—only you can change them. But for change to happen, first you must believe. Without belief, you and I are nothing. Self-doubt is life's biggest hurdle. It was Liliana who challenged me to turn self-doubt into belief. It has worked, and I have never turned back. Many will try to stop you from believing in yourself, even your friends—in my case, even my father—but to find fulfillment, you must follow your own beat."

"But how does Santería come into it? I thought that was your belief, not some religion of the self?"

"It is. Santería, like any religion, is only a way to get in touch with your higher self; it helps you find the path to your true life in this world. In voodoo, Papa Legba is at the crossroads, ready to show you where you are supposed to go. For me it is Elegguá, orisha of roads, and for Luke, Saint Peter. But it doesn't matter what the names are; they give us a place to go when we need to question ourselves. Angéline, I

197

believe you have lost your way, but in your dreams, your inner self is calling out to you. When you were younger you had belief, you had direction and momentum, but you have somehow lost these things.

"Papa Legba has spoken to you, and he has given you guidance in your dreams. He has shown you the beauty in simple things. But Papa Legba and Elegguá are tricksters; they sometimes talk in riddles and show us paradoxes. A simple thing could also be the greatest of things. Like love.

"Luke has not been well, and that has been hard on both of you. He is better now, but he needs you more than ever. You must dance. You must dance, Angéline. You must do simple, beautiful things. Like love."

"Thank you, Pedro. Let's dance together sometime, okay?"

"I would like that."

42

Luke was placing his glass in the dishwasher when the phone rang.

"Luke, it's Alex; good news. The autopsy is back—Buckle died of a stroke, unrelated to the Oxy. The Crown wants to cut a deal as they no longer have a witness to support the charge against you."

"Oh my God." Luke paused to exhale and to give thought to Caleb's death. "What kind of deal?"

"They're dropping all charges against you if you come clean about the mislabeled pills. A good deal, but Dr. Sánchez could be in some serious trouble."

"I've already spoken with her. She sensed this was coming and she's willing to clear up everything."

"Fair enough, then. I'll pass that on to the Crown. Assuming Dr. Sánchez comes through, it looks like you're free."

"Thanks, Alex. I've got to go, Angéline just came in."

"Okay, I'll keep you in the loop."

Luke hung up the phone. He went to the front porch, where Angéline greeted him with a smile as wide as her open arms.

"Angel, I have good news. Alex just told me that all the charges against me have been dropped."

"Oh, Luke—thank God! All of the gods."

"That's the good news. The bad news is that they want to nail Liliana for misrepresenting the medication."

"Oh my."

"Your day, how was it?"

"Let me put it this way: I love you, I'm starting a flamenco dance class and we're going to New Orleans for Mardi Gras."

43

Cutting the deal with the Crown wasn't easy for Luke and it wasn't how Liliana had imagined things turning out, but the most worthwhile goals were usually much more difficult to achieve than they initially seemed. Her life's commitment had been to the health of others and she was unambiguous about what she did. Change was difficult, and sometimes taking a risk was the only way to make it happen. Liliana understood the power of medicine, but the business of medicine was starting to make her sick. The efficacy rates of many medications were often less than sixty percent—time was a better healer. And then there were the side effects and drug interactions that were as nasty as the illness itself, everything from nausea to paralysis to death. Big Pharma spent fourteen billion each year on advertising. Liliana wondered if Big Pharma was just a newer version of the quacksalvers of the past, those who hawked home remedies to the gullible. Only the backyard barn had been replaced by shiny laboratories.

An advertisement for Ambien caught Liliana's eye as she was flipping through a magazine while waiting to speak with Alex Caddigan. Ambien, one of the best-selling selling sleep medications of all time. But there, at the bottom of the page in small print, was a list of more than fifty possible side effects, one of which was "confusion about identity, place and time." Liliana smiled. Sounded like a conspiracy drummed up by psychologists to grab a bigger piece of the health pie.

Cholesterol, diabetes and arthritis drugs were the top sellers, but oxy was drawing the world's attention these days for many reasons.

And now she was in the thick of it. At least, in Newfoundland, her fight would be a fair one. In Cuba, the stench of autocracy got in the way of everything. Even justice, especially justice.

She was not going to retreat in the face of adversity, but confront it head-on, just like Camilo Cienfuegos had done did in 1960 when he witnessed ideology replacing tolerance.

The door to Alex's office opened.

"Come in, Dr. Sánchez."

"Please, call me Liliana."

44

Luke pulled the summons out of his pocket and looked at it to make sure he had the right time. There it was 10 a.m. December 17, Her Majesty the Queen v. Liliana María Sánchez.

The snowflakes were big, which meant they wouldn't accumulate. 'Big snow, little snow" was a common refrain in the oldest city. Luke held out his hand and several flakes floated onto his palm. He turned and offered the pureness to Angéline. Her warm tongue licked away the icy crystals.

"I love you, Luke."

"I love you, Angel."

"Just think, Louisiana in a few months."

"Nice, but we'd better see how the trial goes. Anything could happen."

"True."

Luke looked up as he approached the St. John's Court House, a Romanesque Revival granite and sandstone bastion of law and order. Once it had been the office of the prime minister of Newfoundland, before the country had become a province of Canada. Conical and square turrets framed the building and four giant clocks topped the largest tower. It was 9:45.

Luke knew that a brook still ran through the bedrock in the basement, where the cells were. If they'd been able to hear it, it must have been the sound of freedom to the thousands who had spent long nights in the lockup. Once there'd been a moat, now twenty feet below the surface of the Duckworth Street entrance, where prisoners had taken their exercise. There were ghosts too, springing from stories of crimes, hidden chambers and hangings.

The most serious of indictable offences ended up at the Trial Division of the Supreme Court of Newfoundland and Labrador, which was housed in this courthouse. The charge against Liliana was a lesser indictable offence. These were usually handled in the lower courts, but because Alex had expedited the trial, the Supreme Court was the only space available.

Luke and Angéline began the long climb up the seventy-eight stairs that took them to the Duckworth Street entrance of the courthouse. Luke pointed to the steel door on the side of the building.

"Right in there, Angel, that's where Caleb Buckle spent his last night—in the city lock-up."

Luke reached out for the brass handle on the heavy panelled door of the Duckworth Street entrance to the courthouse. Everything was heavy here. On a plaque at the front of the building were the following words: "The site, scale and design all give the impression of solidarity and power, considered appropriate for its legal and other functions."

A burly sheriff with a razor-sharp brush cut stood at the main entrance, a human embodiment of power. He looked more like a commando than a guard. The only weapon he had was his size, but you'd be a damn fool to mess with that.

"Can I help you?"

"The Sánchez trial," said Luke.

"Courtroom No. 1. Leave your backpack here."

In the entranceway, there were oak panels, exquisite relief carvings and frosted etched glass. A magnificent staircase, the width of twelve men, led to two more levels. The dark oak spindles and thick rails were of another time, a time when quality was the essential point. Luke thought back to the newer courthouse down on Water Street: flimsiness and improvisation had replaced power and solidarity. Progress must have meant different things to different people.

Angéline and Luke passed through the finely carved doorway into Courtroom No. 1. The vastness of the room lent an air of freedom to the place. Four long, arched windows allowed the morning light to flicker on the white walls, enhancing the feeling of openness. Through the windows, Luke could see the grassy hill beside the entrance to the lock-up. As much as this was about Liliana, Luke couldn't shake the face of Caleb Buckle.

Just as Luke and Angéline sat down on an oak bench, Liliana and Pedro stepped through the arched doors. Luke thought they both seemed to take deep breaths upon entering, moved either by the majesty of the place or the gravity of the circumstance. Following behind them, pulling a trolley of cardboard file boxes, was Alex Caddigan, already dressed for trial in his black gown and white collar.

While Liliana and Pedro, who was wearing a long canvas parka with its hood pulled tightly around his head, greeted Luke and Angéline, Alex Caddigan headed directly for the Defence table and began organizing files. The sheriff stepped away from his post at the door and walked towards Pedro. "Please remove your hood, sir."

"Sí." Pedro unpeeled his head from the top of the parka; the sheriff smiled at him. Pedro smiled back. It was different here. The police were your friends. At least that's the way it seemed.

Liliana sat down beside Luke and patted his hand. "Luke, how are you?"

"I'm fine. Are you okay, Liliana?"

"I'm great. Don't worry." She made a face halfway between a grimace and a grin. "But Pedro is returning to Boston in two days. I'll miss him."

"Oh no." Angéline leaned around Luke to look at Pedro.

"We're lucky we got seats," said Luke, looking around the empty, silent room. Besides the people who worked there, the four of them were the only ones present.

But Pedro saw five: with his staff and single red feather above his forehead, Elegguá peered out from behind the coat of arms above the judge's bench.

At precisely ten o'clock the door at the front of courtroom opened. An elderly man with thick white hair and a firm stride walked towards the judge's bench. Glancing to her right, the court clerk, a middle-aged woman with long black hair addressed the courtroom:

"Order, all rise. Judge Thomas J. Murray presiding. Your Honour, we have file number 23478, Her Majesty the Queen v. Dr. Liliana Sánchez."

Only Pedro and Angéline were in the gallery. Potential witnesses like Luke had to wait in the hall. Liliana had already taken her place in the dock, and Alex Caddigan was sitting at his table.

Judge Murray looked up from his long bench and turned to the Crown.

"Good morning, Mr. Strong,"

"Good morning, Justice."

"Mr. Caddigan."

"Good morning, Justice."

"Mr. Caddigan, any Charter challenges?"

"No Charter challenges, Your Honour."

"Thank you, Mr. Caddigan.

"Mr. Strong, opening statements?"

"Your Honour, Dr. Liliana Sánchez is charged under Section 380(1) of the Criminal Code with fraud. And given the conceivable resale value of more than five thousand dollars for the recovered drugs, this is a lesser indictable offence."

"Thank you, Mr. Strong. Go ahead."

"On December 3, at 11:10 a.m., Constable Anne Agnes Cooper and Constable Jonathan Kevin O'Neil of the RNC entered 247 Southside Road. Mr. Luke Delaney and his friend Mr. James Moss, were present at the time."

"Mr. Delaney was charged under the Controlled Drugs and Substances Act with possession for the purpose of trafficking, but those charges have been dropped. However, in the wake of the Delaney investigation, Dr. Sánchez has been charged with fraud.

"While searching Mr. Delaney's residence, a bottle of sixty-two pills was found. Each individual pill was the colour and size of an OxyNEO, and was stamped with ON on one side and 80 on the other. When these pills were sent to the lab, however, it was discovered that they were sugar pills."

"You have witnesses, Mr. Strong. Whom would you like to call first?"

"The Crown calls Inspector Winston Nigel Myrick." The Crown attorney stepped outside the courtroom and returned with Myrick. He stepped into the witness box and took the oath of affirmation: "I solemnly affirm that the evidence to be given by me shall be the truth, the whole truth and nothing but the truth."

"Inspector Myrick, would you please tell the court how you came to arrest Dr. Liliana Sánchez."

"Your Honour, Dr. Sánchez turned herself in to the police on December 13. After the Delaney case was scrapped, Dr. Sánchez came forward to say she had mislabelled the medication, but that she would be pleading not guilty."

"Is Dr. Sánchez in the courtroom now?"

"Yes, that's Dr. Sánchez in the dock."

"Let the court records show that Inspector Myrick pointed to the accused, Dr. Liliana Sánchez."

"Inspector, could you please tell the court about the substance that Dr. Sánchez is accused of mislabelling."

"The plastic pill bottle that was found at the Delaney residence had sixty-two pills inside. The pills were green in colour and were marked ON one side and 80 on the other."

"Could you please tell the court what those letters and numbers represent to you?"

"It seemed obvious that the pills were a Schedule 1 narcotic, oxycodone, specifically OxyNEO."

"And, according to the lab analysis, could you please tell the court, what, in fact, the contents were."

"The contents, Your Honour, were milk sugar. They were sugar pills."

"And from your experience, Inspector Myrick, what do you see as the purpose of the mislabelling?"

"Mislabeling is often a means of creating a false pretense for profit. The street value of a single OxyNEO 80 pill can go as high as eighty dollars, or a dollar per milligram. It only costs a few cents to produce a sugar pill. If you were successful in selling a sugar-pill for an OxyNEO the payoff would be huge. In this case, more than six thousand dollars."

"No more questions, Your Honour."

"Cross-examination, Mr. Caddigan?"

Alex Caddigan got to his feet, looked upwards and scratched his head.

"Inspector Myrick, how long have you been a police officer?"

"Twenty-three years."

"You said in your testimony that mislabelling is often a means of creating a false pretense for profit. Does 'often a means' mean 'always a means,' Inspector?"

"Of course not."

"Well then, what evidence do you have that Dr. Liliana Sánchez intended to sell those pills?"

"None, Mr. Caddigan."

"Thank you, Inspector."

Alex Caddigan shuffled through some papers on his desk.

"One other question, Your Honour. Inspector, do you think sugar pills have any medicinal value?"

Garrett Strong stood up.

"Your Honour, Mr. Caddigan is wasting the Court's time. Inspector Myrick is a police officer, not a pharmacist."

"Mr. Strong, I will be the one who decides if the Court's time is being wasted. Mr. Caddigan, I'm not sure where you are going with this, but, continue—with caution. Answer the question, Inspector."

"I guess I've heard of such things."

"Such things?"

"Like people getting better from taking sugar pills, I suppose."

"Did you consider that when you speculated on Dr. Sánchez intent? Yes or no."

"No."

"No further questions, Your Honour."

"Any more witnesses, Mr. Strong?"

"No further witnesses, Your Honour."

"Mr. Caddigan, please call your first witness."

"Defense calls Luke Aaron Delaney."

Alex Caddigan lawyer left the courtroom and came back with Luke, who entered the witness box.

The court clerk passed Luke a small card. Luke read the contents aloud: "I solemnly affirm that the evidence to be given by me shall be the truth, the whole truth and nothing but the truth."

Alex Caddigan approached the box.

"Mr. Delaney, you are looking well."

"Thank you. I feel great."

"What were your ailments before seeing Dr. Sánchez?"

"Back pain from a car accident in 2005 resulting in an addiction to prescription painkillers. Oxycodone."

"Have you recovered from the back pain and the addiction?"

"Yes, completely."

"Mr. Delaney, did you ever feel you were misled by the accused, Dr. Sánchez?"

"No, Dr. Sánchez was always forthright with me."

"Did any money change hands between you and Dr. Sánchez?"

"Yes, Dr. Sánchez gave me a sum of money."

"How much?"

"Twenty thousand dollars."

"She gave you twenty thousand dollars?"

"Yes."

"And what did she want in return?"

"For me to get well. That's all."

"No more questions, Your Honour."

"Cross-examination, Mr. Strong."

"Mr. Delaney, please tell the court the kinds of symptoms you experienced when you were addicted."

"There were many: insomnia, sweating, irritability, nausea."

"What about confusion and poor judgment?"

"Yes, that too."

"Is it fair to say that you may have been confused and had poor judgment when Dr. Sánchez offered you money to take her pills? Yes or no."

"Well . . ."

"Yes or no, Mr. Delaney."

"Yes, I suppose."

"No further questions, Your Honour."

"Mr. Caddigan, do you have any other witnesses?"

Calling the accused to the witness stand could wreck a case. Or solidify it. If the credibility of the accused was compromised, it could destroy all earlier supportive evidence. Then there was the cross-examination: opening the accused to interrogation could crush the defence.

Alex Caddigan considered the strength of his case. It was just as strong as the Crown's, but he was sure he saw the judge lean forward when Luke owned up to the possibility of being confused. Confusion was often the precursor to coercion, and he was sure that's where Garrett Strong was heading. It was a solid blow; there wasn't much choice.

Caddigan turned and nodded to Liliana.

"Your Honour, the defence calls Dr. Liliana Sánchez."

Liliana opened the gate to the dock and got into the witness box. On her way, she turned and nodded to Angéline and Pedro. She read the solemn affirmation from a card.

Alex Caddigan stood up and approached the box.

"Dr. Sánchez, please tell the court what you do."

"I'm a professor of pharmacology at Memorial University of Newfoundland."

"Where were you born?"

"I was born in Havana, Cuba, but I left there in 1991 and was granted asylum in Canada as a refugee."

"Why did you leave?"

"Freedom. Freedom was a personal quest, and freedom of mind is the lifeblood of my work."

"Your Honour, for the court to understand the work Dr. Sánchez does, a short history would be beneficial."

"Go ahead, Dr. Sánchez."

"Thank you, Your Honour. In World War Two, an anesthesiologist, Dr. Henry Beecher was treating the wounded on the front lines of Africa. Soldiers arrived at the camp hospital with gaping wounds and missing appendages, but some of them didn't seem to be in pain; not initially, anyway.

"Dr. Beecher decided that the body must have its own painkillers. Another thing Dr. Beecher noticed was that the same soldiers winced when getting a needle. It didn't make any sense.

"At one point, Dr. Beecher ran out of morphine to treat the wounded soldiers with, and he injected them with a saline solution instead. To his surprise, their pain disappeared. Your Honour, this was the first recorded example of what we now call the placebo effect—the ability to alter human chemistry by the power of belief. Or expectation."

"Objection, Your Honour, this is ridiculous. A history lesson on fake pills."

"I'd like to hear this out, Mr. Strong. Overruled. Please continue, Dr. Sánchez."

"Your Honour, let me begin by saying that the pharmaceutical world, like its partner the medical world, is still in its infancy in some respects, at least in the sense of what we know as compared to what we don't know. Like an iceberg, I suppose, what we see is but a fraction of what there is. Pain is a complex, multifactorial thing. Yet, we continue to prescribe powerful opiates like OxyNEO, only to replace one kind of pain with another—the pain of addiction. Opiate addiction has become an epidemic. Pain medication is a billion dollar per year industry; the well-being of patients is second to the bottom line.

"I've decided to make a difference. I've been studying the body's ability to manufacture its own medicine. It's called the invisible apothecary."

"Doctor Sánchez, is this what cured Mr. Delaney?"

"Yes, Mr. Caddigan."

"Please explain."

"The body has its own supply of opiates called endorphins. The word *endorphin* means "endogenous morphine," morphine derived from within. We all have it, it's what gives us pleasure and reduces pain. So, my work is all about accessing these endorphins—our own morphine supply. The answer, Your Honour, is through the power of belief. Or expectation. You see, by gaining access to the body's own supply of opiates, we cut off the outside need. The addiction and side effects disappear and so too does the pain. As in Luke Delaney's case."

"Tell the court about belief and expectation."

"If you have unwavering belief and positive expectation, endorphins are released. So, as medical practitioners we make up stories, we use theatre, we encourage, and, yes, we use fake pills to create expectation."

"That's interesting, Dr. Sánchez, but did you say, 'make up stories'?"

"Yes, the story I made up for Luke Delaney was all about a formula that I smuggled in from Cuba. None of it was true, but it made his belief in the sugar pills I gave him stronger. The more evocative the story, the greater the results. So, yes, it's the story, the grandiose story, and the belief in me, that triggered Mr. Delaney's endorphin rush. There are other factors that can improve the placebo effect; injections are more effective than sham pills and sham surgery is better than injections. Even the colour and size of pills can have a measurable effect. And as marketers have known for years, endorsement also adds to the power of belief. As does peer pressure.

"Furthermore, Your Honour, more than a thousand drugs have been taken off the market because they performed no better than a sugar pill. Many believe that for pain, placebo can be close to one hundred percent effective. The more invasive and realistic the sham, the more successful the results. That's exactly where I am with my research, and Luke Delaney is the living example of that."

"One last question, Doctor Sánchez. If your theory works so well, why haven't the big pharmacological companies been all over this?"

"Big Pharma knows all about the placebo effect. It is used in most drug trials. But if it could be proven that we could access the body's own pharmacy in nearly every case to prevent pain and cause healing, how interested would Big Pharma be? This would hardly be profitable to them."

"Thank you, Dr. Sánchez."

"Mr. Strong, do you wish to cross-examine?"

"Yes, Your Honour."

"Dr. Sánchez, you and Mr. Caddigan seemed to have lost track of what this case is all about. This is not about the efficacy of a sugar pill. It's about mislabelling. What's worse, Your Honour, this is about mislabelling a medicine—a product regulated by Health Canada. Well, at least until Dr. Sánchez came along. Furthermore, by Dr. Sánchez's own admission, not only has she fabricated pills but also a story intended to mislead a patient. Your Honour, Dr. Sánchez is not a medical doctor, she's a pharmacologist. She has no right to prescribe anything. Mislabelling a medication is one thing, but mislabelling it as a Schedule I narcotic is far more serious.

"Whenever the police see a pill bottle without a label, like the one Dr. Sánchez has admitted to owning, it usually means that the contents are being manipulated for nefarious reasons."

"Objection."

"Overruled."

Alex Caddigan pulled a pill bottle from his pants pocket. "Your Honour, I take a pile of pills each day. I've put them in a clear pill bottle that I bought at the pharmacy. That hardly makes me a criminal. Mr. Strong's suggestion is conjecture."

"Sustained. Continue, Mr. Strong."

"Your Honour, Dr. Sánchez took advantage of Luke Delaney when he was most vulnerable, when he was in a state of confusion and his judgement was impaired."

Pedro Cienfuegos leapt to his feet. Everything was at a crossroads: belief and disbelief, mind and matter, fiction and truth, conditioning and expectation, consciousness and unconsciousness, chaos and law, right and wrong. Only Pedro could see Elegguá and only Pedro could hear his words. But he would tell them all what wise Elegguá had said.

"Let her pass, she has done no wrong!"

"Sheriff, remove that man from the courtroom."

Garrett Strong's final remarks seemed to evaporate after the outburst.

"Mr. Caddigan. Closing remarks?"

"Thank you, Your Honour. I remember from math class that if you multiply a number by zero the result is always zero."

Garrett Strong rolled his eyes. *Here we go.*

"Your Honour, the pills in question are inert. They have a value of zero. So how can Dr. Sánchez be guilty of anything if the product was no more than zero to begin with.

"As for the OC stamped on the pills, that could mean anything. In this case, Your Honour, OC stands for Olivia Cienfuegos, which is the name of Dr. Sánchez's aunt. Ms. Cienfuegos was the inspiration for Dr. Sánchez's lifelong work.

"Mr. Delaney is not a victim of fraud, Your Honour: no money was taken from him. On the contrary, Mr. Delaney made money."

"Dr. Sánchez is a scholar. One who is on track to changing the pharmaceutical industry forever. Your Honour, you see Luke Delaney here, healthy and well, a living example of Dr. Sánchez's work.

"In conclusion, Your Honour, we shouldn't be charging Dr. Sánchez, we should be celebrating her accomplishments.

"The Defence rests."

"Thank you, Mr. Caddigan. Court will adjourn until two thirty."

"All rise."

Judge Murray collected his papers and exited through a door at the front of the courtroom. Liliana Sánchez turned to Alex Caddigan and extended her hand. "How do you think it went?"

"This case is all about reasonable doubt, Liliana. I'd be surprised if the decision doesn't go your way. But you never know. Whatever the case, I like what you do and I meant to tell you before this that I am handling the case pro bono."

"Does that include coffee too?"

"Sure, why not? We've got a few hours before the verdict."

"Shall we invite the gang?"

Alex and Liliana turned and looked behind them: Pedro had returned to the courtroom and was pointing to the coat of arms on the wall.

"Oh my. It's Elegguá again. He's seeing Elegguá up there."

"What in God's name is an Elegguá?"

"A deity of his religion. One of the most important ones."

"I'm not into all that stuff."

"But we just tried to prove what the power of belief can do, didn't we?"

"Sure, but that was about fake pills, not fake god. Anyway, all gods are fake."

Liliana approached the empty witness box and pointed her finger at it.

"Mr. Caddigan, your world is all about doubt—reasonable doubt. For me, doubt is the curse of all curses."

Judge Murray walked to the bench with a sheaf of papers, sat down and cleared his throat. "I find that the Crown is not in possession of enough evidence to proceed with the case against Dr. Sánchez. You are discharged, Dr. Sánchez."

Luke and Angéline stepped hand in hand onto the slippery grass on the slope beside the concrete steps that led to Water Street. The snow had stopped falling, and the sun peered out from behind a cloud.

The shadows of a man and a dog moved along an adjacent wall. As quickly as they appeared, they vanished again. Then, suddenly, the dog appeared in the flesh, running towards Luke in full stride, his tail swirling like a lasso, eyes bulging.

"Blackjack!"

The dog's momentum knocked Luke and Angéline to the ground. Blackjack howled in delight. His eyes were like polished onyx with flashes of light splitting the darkness. Luke was sure he saw Caleb Buckle in the blackness of his dog's eyes. A piece of paper was sticking out of the zippered opening on Blackjack's collar. Luke carefully removed it and unfolded the perfectly creased sheet. Only a blind man could fold something with such perfection, feeling the corners like they were the edges of a precipice. But the writing was a mess, the intertwined letters barely discernable. Luke pondered it and then spoke:

"There are things known and there are things unknown, and in between are the doors of perception."

Angéline LeBlanc touched Luke's neck. It was a gentle touch, lighter than a snowflake, but somehow it carried all the love she had for him.

Luke took his hat, his beautiful hat, and placed it on her head.